Jim Cockin enjoyed writing stories when he was growing up in the Midlands. When he became a journalist he got to write them every day. He worked on television news programmes for ITV and the BBC and then became a reporter at Sky Sports. There he covered everything from Premier League football and England's Lionesses to cricket, boxing and darts. He has also produced TV documentaries about theatre and ballet and worked in the communications industry.

He has never seen a ghost, but would like to.

GHOST TIDE

JIM COCKIN

Published in 2024
by Lightning
Imprint of Eye Books Ltd
29A Barrow Street
Much Wenlock
Shropshire
TF13 6EN

www.eye-books.com

ISBN: 9781785633775

Cover illustration by Martha Vine, design and layout by Nell Wood

Typeset in Iowan Old Style and Broadsheet

British Library Cataloguing in Publication Data
A catalogue record for this book is available from the British Library.

For my mother and father

'What's past is prologue...'
The Tempest

PROLOGUE

East coast of England, 1897
Serpent's Tongue rocks

People had drowned. He could tell as much from the weary beat of the lifeboat's oars as the little craft emerged from the mist and spray. The lighthouse keeper set down the basket of logs by the door of his cottage and squinted out to sea, cursing his failing eyes. The bark of a dog carried on the winter wind and moments later a collie came bounding over the headland towards him, a stick clamped between its jaws.

'No time to play now, Jed,' the lighthouse keeper said.

Sensing the mood, the dog fell into step behind his master, following him over the scrubland towards the water's edge and the lighthouse tower.

For many years the lighthouse had stood guard over the notorious Serpent's Tongue rocks which curled like a snake out into the cold waters of the North Sea. They were unique on this stretch of coastline, which was better known for its shifting shingle and retreating cliffs. Their geology shaped the currents here in treacherous and unpredictable ways, scouring out deep underwater trenches and piling up deadly sandbanks just offshore. The keeper hurried on towards the tower, the wind pulling at his shaggy beard and oilskin jacket.

Inside, the roar of the gale died instantly as he slammed the heavy door behind them. The dog scampered ahead up the spiral staircase, his bark echoing off the walls, and on towards the lamp room, paws ticking over each stone step as he passed. There was a time when the lighthouse keeper would have raced his dog, but now his bones were heavy with the years.

The staircase opened into a circular room where a great oil lamp stood raised on a platform. When day darkened to dusk, he could always be found here, lighting the lamp and tending the flame, each night adding another thin layer to the coat of smoke and soot that streaked the walls. Anxiously he picked up his telescope and turned it out to sea. Sharpening the focus, he could pick out the faces of the returning lifeboat crew at their oars. Yes, he was there – his own son was safe! But the keeper could tell from the grim set of the lad's face that terrible things must have happened that day. He put down the telescope and murmured a prayer of thanks.

The alarm had been raised earlier that morning: a steamship in trouble just offshore on the Serpent's Teeth sandbank, with a furious gale raging. The bells had clanged urgently across the town and his son George had answered the call like so many others in Dunstrand: the farm hands had looked up from the fields and laid down their shovels; the baker's boy had abandoned his sacks of flour in the yard; the fishermen on the quay had thrown down their nets and all of them had gone running down to the shore and the lifeboat. Their courage always humbled him.

———◇———

'We did all that we could,' George said, later that evening.

They sat at the kitchen table, a fire snapping in

the grate. The lighthouse keeper listened attentively, his eyes fixed on the flames and the dog nuzzling at his feet.

'She was a small passenger steamship, on the run over from Holland or Belgium, I think,' his son continued. 'She was called *Miranda*. Looked as if she'd had a fire on board. By the time we reached her, she'd already been driven up onto the sandbanks by the storm. She had no power and the current had squared her up to the waves. She was starting to break up. We could see people on the deck, trying to climb higher to escape the water. Some were in the rigging, but their hands must have been so frozen, they couldn't hold on. I saw two people fall. One was a child.'

The lighthouse keeper reached across the table and laid his hand over his son's for a moment. It still felt chill.

'We tried to get closer to secure a line, but the wind was whipping up the waves,' the young man continued. 'More passengers kept coming up from below. I remember one woman. She just stood there, terrified, holding this bundle of blankets in her arms. Then I saw the bundle kick and I realised it was her baby, all wrapped up. And the waves kept pounding the ship, washing over the deck, and we all knew we didn't have much time until the *Miranda* was broken up or was driven clean off the sandbank and capsized into the deeper water beyond.'

He paused, transfixed by the memory. The dog turned in a restless circle and found a new position closer to the fire.

'And then something strange happened. We were turning our boat around to try again to get in close, when a man appeared on deck. Where he had been all this time, I don't know; but now he seemed to take charge. He stood out from the rest of them: tall and slim, dressed in a black coat with long dark hair blowing about his shoulders. The way he moved set him apart. Like he was calm; not frightened of anything. He helped the young woman and her baby along the deck towards the last remaining lifeboat and cut it free. Then he went back for more passengers, guiding them along the deck and taking command. And all the time the waves were pounding the ship and there was this fearful sound of buckling metal and the sea was thick with oil and grease. I saw bodies in the water too; they were beyond help.'

The candle on the table guttered. The lighthouse keeper kept his eyes on the fire as his son continued his story.

'We made one last effort to get close to them, but another wave lifted us up and for a moment I swear I thought we would all be be drowned. But our boat righted itself and the wave broke over the deck of the *Miranda*. She had water streaming from every surface and I remember hearing a scream on the wind. Somehow they had managed to get their lifeboat away and I saw it riding the waves on our starboard side. Poor souls. They looked half dead already, soaked and frozen. We changed course to help them but as we turned, something made me look back at the *Miranda*.

'I could see the tall man dragging a travelling case up from the hold. It was bound with heavy leather straps. Another wave struck the ship and I swear I saw her shudder, as if she were on the brink of rolling over. But here was the curious thing. There was nothing about that man's movements that showed any hint of fear. He was fixed only on hauling his case steadily up to the bow of the ship. Then there came another terrible boom of breaking metal that would have scared the devil himself, and through the spray I saw the man pause, silhouetted against the raging sea. Then he lifted his case high above his head and with enormous strength, hurled it as far as he could out into the deeper water. For a moment it bobbed on the surface, before another huge wave hit the ship and rolled it off the sandbank, capsizing it into the sea. I watched for that man but he never reappeared. And a few moments later there was no sign of him, the ship – or anyone else.'

George sat silent for a moment, his story spent; and when the lighthouse keeper looked up from the glowing coals, he saw his son's face was streaked with tears.

CHAPTER ONE

Charlie scowled at his mother through the train window, his forehead pressed against the cold glass. She waved back at him from the platform in an exaggerated display of enthusiasm which he refused to acknowledge, instead staring sullenly beyond her as the carriage pulled out of Liverpool Street station. He yanked his headphones from his jacket pocket and set down his phone on the plastic table. How could she actually have done this? He could probably report her to the authorities: it was borderline child cruelty.

The train creaked like the bones of an old man as it began to move, and the platform gave way to the grimy backs of graffiti-covered buildings. Dirty plants sprouted from holes in the brickwork and streaks of rain started to roll down the window. Swallowed by a sudden tunnel, the glass darkened and Charlie caught a glimpse of his own reflection: spiky blond hair that made him look as if he had just suffered a mild electric shock, soft blue eyes, pale skin and a snub nose rimmed red with the remains of an end-of-term cold. He looked in need of a good rest, but thanks to his mother there was now no chance of that. A message buzzed on his phone from Sanjay, suggesting a pizza at lunchtime. Charlie tapped out his reply and his friend's response was a gratifying mix of outrage and sympathy.

The train gathered speed, pushing between flats and offices. Every balcony and window seemed to be decorated with sagging strings of tinsel and coloured lights. A neon-lit shopping centre glowed in the gloom and the streets alongside the railway were jammed with cars, their windscreen wipers beating back and forth. It was the sort of day that couldn't be bothered to get light and Charlie stared blankly as it all rolled by: the Christmas holidays weren't supposed to be like this.

The previous day he had come home from school so excited that he had done a knee-slide along the hallway like a footballer celebrating an injury-time winner. The longest term was over. No more hauling himself out of bed at seven every morning, no more percentages or poetry; no more homework, lunch queues, tests, checks, rules or Joe Dixon and his bullying gang – just pleasing himself. But all that joy had evaporated. And it was his mother's fault.

The tannoy crackled into life, listing items for sale in the buffet car. Charlie's fingers closed around the twenty-pound note that she had thrust into his pocket on the concourse. Guilt money. Still, perhaps some food would be welcome under the circumstances.

The smell of hot bacon and instant coffee hit him as he swayed into the next carriage. Behind a steel counter was a short man with a tuft of ginger hair that made him look a like a carrot. A badge on his waistcoat said 'ERIC – HAPPY TO HELP' but, judging by his weary expression, Charlie thought that was probably unlikely.

'What can I get you?' Eric sounded as if he too was recovering from a heavy cold.

Charlie looked up at the menu on the wall, determined to spend too much of his mother's money in a tiny act of revenge.

'A bacon and sausage roll, please. And a chocolate bar. And a cup of tea. Have you got any crisps?'

Eric shuffled slowly around his kitchenette, dropping the items one by one into a paper bag and opening the microwave.

'That's a big breakfast you're having this morning.'

'It's probably my lunch as well,' said Charlie. 'I've got a long journey.'

'Where you going?'

'Place called Dunstrand. Up on the east coast. Miles away.'

Eric directed a jet of hot water from the machine into a plastic cup. 'In that case, you'll need to change trains at Ipswich for Brampton. Then it's either a taxi or a very long walk. Milk and sugar's over there.'

You need to change trains. Charlie's mother had told him the same thing about a million times in the past twenty-four hours. That and the thing about 'fresh air' being good for you. Not as good for you as hanging out with your mates at home to recover from a busy school term, but Dr Mills was not interested in her son's protests. She had used the special voice she usually reserved for dealing with her difficult patients in the hospital A&E: 'You are not spending a week unsupervised loafing around shopping centres and playing video games. You are only just fourteen, for heaven's sake! I can't leave you on your own! It's not my fault the night shift is short-staffed this week. That's how life goes sometimes. Plans change.

Sometimes we all have to... What's that charming phrase of yours? Suck it up.'

The bacon roll oozed hot fat as Charlie sank his teeth into it. Flat brown fields unfurled beyond the train window; a solitary tractor surrounded by birds flashed by.

His dad had been no help either, Charlie reflected bitterly. It had been a snatched conversation, his father pausing on some shimmering construction site in a faraway desert to take the video call and offer only sympathy to his son and support for his wife. Removing his sunglasses to wipe away a trickle of sweat that had leaked out from under his hard hat, Mr Mills had simply repeated the mantra that he so often used when he was working away: 'Your mother's in charge: what she says, goes.' He would be back in a week, he had said, and was happy to come and collect Charlie on Christmas Eve, which was not really any help at all. Then the picture froze and the call dropped, leaving Charlie protesting vainly at an empty screen.

The train stopped briefly and a handful of passengers bustled aboard. A stout lady in a headscarf, pulling a yapping dog on a lead, made her way towards him and Charlie shifted uneasily in his seat. Ever since a black Labrador had bounded up to him in the park when he was five and knocked him flat on his back, he had been deeply suspicious of all animals, and dogs in particular. His anxiety was made all the worse by the inevitable insistence of the owner that the dog was 'just being friendly', even as it jumped up and licked your hand with filthy hot saliva. Charlie had cried for half an hour that day and had to be carried home by his mum.

The lady moved towards him. 'This seat free?' The dog started to bark and snuffle round the aisle.

'It is,' said Charlie, getting up.

He gathered the remains of his meal, hauled down his suitcase from the rack and moved to the far end of the train. It was hard work dragging it along the aisle because his arm was still bruised from that nasty incident in the school playground, but he was trying to put all that out of his mind for now. He found a quiet seat by the window and settled in.

In half an hour it would be time to change. He yawned and a thought struck him: what would happen if he didn't? Perhaps he could ignore the connection he was supposed to make and simply go back to London? That would give his mother a shock. Serve her right. Just turn round and come straight back. But wouldn't he need to buy a new ticket? He wasn't sure he had enough money. Reluctantly, he concluded the idea was too fraught with problems to be carried through.

The change of trains was simple enough and eventually he found himself in a deserted carriage rocking gently along a branch line through the winter fields. In half an hour he would reach the station at Brampton where, according to Mum, his Uncle Patrick would be waiting for him.

He had been trying to remember his uncle, but the picture was hazy. He could vaguely recall a picnic on a beach somewhere and a chocolate cake with sprinkles on the icing. Someone's birthday, maybe? He couldn't think whose. He remembered his dad in a deckchair and Uncle Patrick kneeling in the sand nearby working intently with a little yellow spade to create an octopus sculpture with strings of seaweed for tentacles. Actually, perhaps Charlie wasn't remembering it at all. Maybe he was thinking of that photograph in the album beside Mum's bed. There was definitely a shot of his uncle on a beach, giving a peace sign to the camera and grinning from under a thick beard and long hair. Whenever it was, it must have been taken before Patrick went away to live in India with his wife. Now she was dead and Patrick and his daughter were back in England. What was Charlie supposed to say to them about it all? His mother had been no use, vaguely talking about remembering to 'show some empathy' and sounding like that counsellor who visited the school each term offering to talk to the class about 'issues'. Charlie could think of nothing worse. Maybe the whole subject would just not come up. All best avoided if possible.

The train shuddered to a stop. Surely this couldn't be right? It didn't look like any station he had seen before. The platform was narrow and empty. In Charlie's experience, stations were noisy places full of busy people going places. All this one had was a postbox.

Reluctantly, he dragged his case through the doors. The air smelt fresh and damp. There was just one bar of signal on his phone and a faint panic began to creep across his chest as the train pulled away.

Where was everyone?

A distant car horn sounded and a dirty Land Rover appeared at the end of the road, its tattered canvas roof flapping like an injured bird trying to take off. It clattered to a halt and a man leaned out of the window, grinning. His beard was neatly trimmed and heavily flecked with grey. His hair was pulled back into a tight ponytail and his face was deeply lined around the eyes, as if it had cracked under the glare of a hot sun. Despite the passage of the years, Charlie recognised him straightaway as the man in the photograph.

'Welcome to the edge of the map, Charlie. Here be dragons after this. Hop in. How was your journey?'

Charlie slammed the door feeling vaguely confused. 'Long. Thanks for picking me up, Uncle Patrick.' He held out his hand.

His uncle looked at it, amused for a moment, then shook it firmly. His skin was coarse and his grip was firm.

'My sister is bringing up a little gentleman.'

Charlie wasn't sure what he was supposed to say to that, but his uncle was already grinding the gears and the Land Rover lurched off down the road.

'I like your car.'

'I'm borrowing it from the Coopers up at the farm while I get myself properly settled. Don't worry about the seat belt. There isn't one.'

As they picked up speed, Uncle Patrick took his hands off the wheel to rummage in the pockets and fished out a packet of tobacco, oblivious to Charlie's alarm.

'Southwold, Walberswick and Aldeburgh are all back that way. You've probably heard of some of them,' he said. 'But we're going to be heading the other way up the coast. Dunstrand is a bit more off the beaten track. You'll see the sea in a little while and then it's only a mile or so to the house.' He nudged the steering wheel with his thighs and rolled a cigarette with his hands. 'Won't take us long.'

'Do you live in Dunstrand?'

'Our house is up at the other end of the beach from the town. Not far, but out on our own a bit. Rush hour for us is when the cows come in for milking.'

Charlie gripped the door handle tighter. The emptiness of it all was starting to make him feel uneasy. A clump of silver birch trees flashed by. Stripped of their leaves, they looked like the bones of a hand pointing at the sky.

'It suits us being so remote,' said Uncle Patrick, taking hold of the wheel once more. 'Years ago I spent a week walking on the east coast. Just me, a backpack, a guidebook and a leaky tent. I think it imprinted itself on my mind somehow, so when we came back from India this was the first place I thought about.

And after all that time we had spent living out there, I could never have survived in a little box flat in a city somewhere. I'd have gone mad. I needed space.'

'So how are you finding being back in England?'

'It's not been...straightforward. But it's been good to be tucked away out here. Nobody really ever passes through and I prefer to keep my head down without being bothered by anyone.'

'But what do you do out here all day?'

A smile curled around his uncle's lips. 'I'm still an artist. Or trying to be.'

He blew a stream of smoke out of the window and then offered the cigarette to Charlie, who shook his head. He had a sudden sensation that the week ahead might be more interesting than he had first imagined.

'Dunstrand is an ancient place,' continued his uncle. 'Some families here can trace their roots back to the Domesday Book. And I think you'll like where we're living. It's practically falling down, which is how we can afford the rent, but there's loads of space for my studio. I'm trying to make a go of the business side of things now we're back in England.'

Tall reeds swayed beside the road and, as they rounded the bend, Charlie suddenly saw the wide sweep of the sea and a huddle of flint-fronted houses scattered along the shore.

'That's Dunstrand,' said his uncle. 'See that lighthouse at the end of the headland? That overlooks the Serpent's Tongue rocks – you can see them sticking out into the sea. Freak of geology. The only hard rock for miles around and it creates some vicious tides and currents. You might want to give the swimming a miss this week. And on a clear day you can see the sandbanks offshore – they're called the Serpent's Teeth.'

Charlie thought his uncle must have spent a lot of time with that guidebook in his leaky tent.

'You can get down to to the beach easily enough from our place. Then it's a nice walk if the tide's out.' He hesitated. 'Maybe you and Ariel would like to try it sometime this week.'

He was silent for a moment and Charlie thought he saw a shadow of concern pass over his uncle's face.

'Can you remember your cousin?' Uncle Patrick asked.

'No, not really. Mum says we were only babies when we met.'

Uncle Patrick stared straight ahead. 'Well, Ariel's at school today. Last day of term. Won't be back until later. You may find her a bit...distant. Remember, it's been a big change for her, coming back after all those years abroad. And it's taken a long time for her to adjust to everything that happened...losing her mother.'

Charlie squirmed in his seat, pretending suddenly to be absorbed in the passing scenery. His uncle stared ahead, rubbing his beard.

'Sometimes this universe makes no sense at all, Charlie. No sense at all.'

They were passing the edge of town now. Narrow streets of crooked cottages ran down to a stone harbour and Charlie caught a glimpse of a market square with a tall Christmas tree in the centre. A pub, a church hall and a tiny supermarket slid by, then the road rose above wide dunes and a long beach where ribbons of sand, twisting in the wind, raced each other along the water's edge. The salt smell was strong here as if the air was coming from far away, clean and unused.

'Nearly there.'

They passed between thin hedges and low trees bent by the constant sea breeze, then swung up a tiny pot-holed lane and turned sharply left between two red brick gateposts and into a wide gravelled drive.

'Welcome to Darkwater House!'

They sat in silence, the engine ticking.

In front of them was the most decrepit and overgrown old house that Charlie had ever seen. It took him a few moments even to distinguish the outline of the roof and walls, so thick were the ivy and creeper surging up one side. It looked as if the garden was trying to eat the house. The upper windows, set high in the walls, reflected back the grey of the sky. Several slates were missing from the roof. Great green patches of moss and lichen had spread unevenly across the façade, making it look as if someone had flung an army camouflage net over the entire house in an effort to hide it from view. A long, low extension jutted out to one side and, from an incongruously modern steel chimney, a trail of sweet-smelling wood smoke danced in the wind. A ragged holly hedge, studded with bright red berries, encircled the ground floor, breaking only to reveal a lopsided portico and a faded blue front door.

Charlie could feel his uncle drinking in his discomfort. A mischievous smile spread over Patrick's face. 'It's even worse inside.'

CHAPTER TWO

Charlie chewed slowly on a cheese sandwich, the springs of the mattress underneath him protesting at every bite. Cheese, no meat: Mum had neglected to tell him they were vegetarian at Darkwater House. He was glad of the chocolate bar from the train.

He looked round his tiny bedroom, scarcely able to take in his new surroundings. Not that there was much to see: a plain desk, a chair and a wardrobe with a tarnished, full-length mirror attached. Wedges of yellowing newspaper protruded from beneath the feet of the wardrobe in a forlorn effort to combat the alarming slope of the floor.

His mind ran back over the hour since he had crossed the threshold and into that echoing hall. 'I thought we'd put you right up on the top deck,' his uncle had said, leading the way. 'You can even see the sea – when it's not raining.'

The tour of the house had been a blur of dim passageways and dusty, shut-up rooms. In a downstairs study, an old ginger cat had made Charlie jump when it suddenly appeared on the top of a bookcase, eyeing him with suspicion.

'Don't mind Ferdinand,' Uncle Patrick had said. 'He was living here way before any of us.'

They had then peered into a series of musty rooms, all faded curtains, thin carpet and thick dust. It put Charlie in mind of the school history trip at the start of term when they had visited a house used by the government for secret operations in the Second World War. Like Darkwater, it had been simple, sparse and virtually untouched since the 1930s.

He swallowed the last mouthful of his sandwich and leaned back against the headboard. The deep silence of the house wrapped itself around him and he felt it tightening like a belt. He thought of his own bedroom back in London, alive with the swish of traffic outside and the faint clattering of trains towards town; a place in perpetual motion, humming to itself, comforting him with the familiar beat of its pulse. But out here? A week at the edge of the map with people he barely knew? A tear slid down his cheek.

He had to get outside.

Unzipping his case, Charlie chucked his clothes onto the bed and found a jacket, a pair of gloves and his blue beanie. He hurried downstairs, desperate to get away from the oppressive gloom of his own room. But as he passed one of the closed doors on the landing, he stopped.

From inside he heard the faint sound of laughter. He paused and listened. It was a child's voice. It rippled once more, and then, as if a joke were being shared, it was joined by another laugh: two voices together, a boy and a girl, no more than four or five years old.

Charlie frowned. Perhaps someone else was here in Darkwater House with his uncle and cousin? The place was certainly big enough for lodgers. Or maybe Ariel was back from school earlier than expected. There was a simple way to find out.

He tapped on the door.

No reply.

Charlie knocked more firmly this time, but again there was no answer, so he turned the handle and stepped inside.

The room was empty.

All he could see was a single bed covered in a

dust sheet, a fireplace and a dead bluebottle on the windowsill. It looked as if no one had been in there for years. Charlie frowned and hurried on downstairs. Had he just imagined the laughter? It was possible. It had been a long day already and he was hardly feeling himself. Anyway, everyone knew old houses made strange noises. That was probably it. It didn't do to think too much about these things when you weren't feeling right.

He was going to mention it to Uncle Patrick but, as he approached the kitchen, he checked himself. It was hard enough spending the week with relatives he barely knew, let alone getting things off on the wrong foot by making them think he was some sort of weirdo who heard noises in empty rooms.

'All settled in?' Uncle Patrick was filling the kettle at a vast sink. The kitchen was large and by the far the warmest room in the house, with a log-burning stove smouldering away beside a range cooker amid a confusion of pots, pans, and plates. Charlie stretched out his hands to the fire.

'Uncle Patrick, what's the wi-fi code here?'

'There isn't one. We don't have it. There's a café in Dunstrand where I go if I need to get online.'

Charlie was appalled. This was not just another

place but another time.

'We do have a landline. You're welcome to use that.' Uncle Patrick took a herbal tea bag from a tin beside the kettle. 'Now, a word about tomorrow morning. We need to be down in Dunstrand by six and I'm going to need your help.'

'What with?'

'It's the Christmas Market and I have a stall there. It'll be an early start, but it should be a good day. I'm coming to realise it's better to be an artist who sells things rather than one who doesn't.' He looked out of the window, lost in thought. 'You could get away with that abroad, but life's a bit more complicated here. Rent. Council tax. That sort of thing.'

The snap of the boiled kettle brought him back to the present.

'The next few days are going to be busy for me, Charlie. First the Dunstrand market, then another on the other side of Norfolk later in the week. They can't get enough of my hand-painted reindeer mugs at this time of year. Picasso really missed a trick there. Come on, I'll show you the studio.'

Charlie followed him out of the back door.

'These were all stables and barns once.' Uncle Patrick waved at three outhouses which formed a courtyard behind the house with a little paddock just visible beyond. 'It's perfect for me now.'

The latch squeaked and he led Charlie into a whitewashed room that reeked of turpentine and tobacco. A large easel stood in one corner, a half-finished landscape stretched across it, while the rest of the room was jammed from floor to ceiling with shelves full of paint pots, brushes and dirty rags. Beside the window was a table crowded with row upon row of glazed white china mugs.

'Thirty-six reindeer to paint on each one of those by tomorrow morning.' Uncle Patrick took a cheerful swig of tea. 'I'm already seeing the damn things in my sleep.'

'Do you do them all by hand?'

Uncle Patrick switched on a three-bar electric heater that was mounted on the wall and grinned. 'That's what makes it art.'

'Can I help?'

'No, but it's kind of you to offer. If I were you, I'd head off to the beach while it's still light. Take a look around. Get to know the place. Go through the back gate at the end of the garden and follow the path. I hear you can sometimes get a bit of signal on the dunes towards the lighthouse if you want to let your mum know you've arrived.'

With that, he hoisted a crate of mugs from the table and set them out on his workbench. Charlie left him hunched over them, cigarette drooping from his lips, brush held with surprising delicacy between his fingers and Christmas carols drifting from the radio on the windowsill.

Charlie made a brief circuit of the garden, looking for the path to the sea. Behind one hedge he found a vegetable patch with an upturned wheelbarrow and the white ash of a bonfire still smoking beside it. Charlie had never seen a garden so big. He thought of the tiny backyard at home, identical to all the others in their terraced street, with his dad's bike squeezed up against the recycling bins. What did people do with all this space out here? Store junk, by the look of it. The biggest of the outbuildings was piled high with the stuff and the smell of mould made his nostrils twitch. He poked idly among the contents of a dusty wicker basket. It was an unpromising collection: a jumble of broken umbrellas and wooden tennis rackets. But then something caught his eye because it was in far better condition than anything else: a metal detector, complete with headphones and a shoulder strap. Someone must have charged it up recently, because when he turned the dial on the front a light glowed green. On a whim, he slung it over his shoulder and set off down the track to the beach.

The path wound gently downhill, hedgerows on either side. Skipping around the muddy puddles, he arrived at the top of a grassy field with the sea beyond. A herd of cows stood chewing beside a gate on the far side. Charlie hurried over the stile and down onto the beach.

The sea was a long way off, the wet sand crisscrossed with pools and channels cut by the retreating tide. Here and there, flocks of white birds huddled together among the seaweed and stones.

To his right he could see Dunstrand in the distance; to his left the old lighthouse and that headland...what had his uncle called it? The Serpent's Tongue? He could see why. A sliver of black rock thrust out into the sea, forked like the tongue of a snake and every now and then the waves would crash together between the V, sending a plume of spray high into the air. A modern bell-buoy bobbed off shore, warning of the danger with a distant chime and a blinking light.

Charlie set out towards the lighthouse. To liven

up the walk, he unstrapped the metal detector and switched it on. The headphones replaced the sound of the wind with a steady hiss of static. He made his way along the sand, moving the device in a gentle arc in front of him as he had seen people do on the History Channel, something his mum forced him to watch, usually in response to another bang-average school report. It was surprisingly soothing to focus on the tiny world of pebbles and crab claws at his feet rather than the vast beach all around. Cocooned in static, he had not gone far when the machine let out its first beep. He set it down quickly, scrabbling in the wet sand to look for the source. It turned out to be a broken cigarette lighter. By the time he reached the dunes, he had added a ten-pence piece and two beer bottle-tops to his collection. Pleased with his efforts, Charlie pulled out his phone.

No signal.

Undeterred, he climbed to the top of the tallest dune, waving the phone about above his head. Eventually he found a spot with two bars. He sent his mother a single-word text – 'Here' – and then put his phone away without waiting for a reply.

A couple of dog walkers had appeared down by the water's edge. He was glad they were a good distance away as the animals were off their leads and racing in and out of the sea. Close by, at the foot of one of the dunes, a recent storm had scoured out a huge tide-pool just below the high-water mark of driftwood and seaweed. The light was starting to fade and, although he had no intention of getting stuck out here in the dark, the pool intrigued him. It was deep and the sand around it had been gouged smooth by the tide.

He switched on the metal detector and began a slow circuit around the pool, taking care to keep his feet dry. Immediately, a series of rapid beeps filled his headphones, much louder than anything he had heard before. Something was buried at the edge of the tide-pool and, judging by the noise reverberating in his ears, this was more than just the forgotten odds and ends of some distant summer picnic. This was something bigger.

Much bigger.

CHAPTER THREE

The sand was cold against his skin as Charlie dug down with his fingers. The surface of the pool furrowed in the wind. He worked fast and, after a few moments, with a pile of sloppy wet sand beside him, his hands touched the outline of something buried half a metre down. He traced the edge of a hard rectangle, about the size of his school pencil case. With some effort, he wrenched it free.

It was a box, tarnished with seawater and age. Grains of sand coated every indentation of its surface. Gently, he wiped at it with his sleeve and then dipped it into the icy water of the pool before shaking it dry. The box was heavy, made of brass, he guessed, and decorated with an elaborate design. Looking closely, he could see a tree carved into the lid. It had wide branches and a trunk split halfway down to create a cavity, inside which a tiny figure writhed in agony, its arms pinned to the sides of its wooden prison, its mouth contorted in a silent scream. Tentatively, Charlie shook the box, but it made no sound and the clasp at the front refused to move when he pulled at it with his frozen fingers. He tried again, but he could not shift it. The lock was seized shut.

Charlie rubbed at the box with his thumb, brushing away the last of the sand, and down one side he noticed some words, carved in italics and worn smooth by the sea. He traced them with his finger and spoke them out loud:

'All the devils are here.'

A flock of gulls suddenly burst up from behind the dunes, screeching in alarm.

Startled, Charlie watched as they flew over his head. At that moment, further down the beach, he caught sight of a horse and rider galloping over the sand towards him. The horse's dark mane was flowing behind it and its ears were pinned back as it raced through the tide-pools, spray flying from its hooves, the rider hunched low over the reins. Charlie stuffed the box into his jacket pocket, without taking his eyes off the horse and rider. For a while it looked as if they would charge on past. Then, with growing unease, he realised they had altered course and were heading straight for him.

Charlie stood paralysed for a moment, then a survival instinct kicked in and he ran for the shelter of the dunes, not daring to look back. The thunder of the horse grew louder and in desperation he hurled himself down behind a ridge of sand and grass. He lay there, chest heaving, looking up at the reddening sky. Gradually he felt confident enough to peer back at the beach.

The horse had slowed down, the rider forcing it to circle back around in a loop as if preparing for another pass. Jet black and powerful, it let out a wild snort and shook its mane as the rider kicked its flanks, once more aiming it directly at Charlie's hiding place.

He felt better protected this time. He could see what was coming and he knew the sand was too soft and too steep for the horse to climb at any speed. He pressed himself tight to the ground and watched the horse continue its charge.

Then, unexpectedly, the rider leaned back in the saddle and tugged on the reins to slow the beast down, coming to a halt just short of where Charlie lay looking into the low sun. He raised his hands to shield his eyes; horse and rider were a single silhouette against the sky.

'What do you want?' he called. His voice sounded shrill.

The rider laughed. 'Did I scare you?'

'A little bit.'

'Good!'

The horse stepped forward a pace and the rider slipped down gracefully from the saddle; long black hair fell loose as she removed her hat. The eyes that measured him were filled with a haughty disdain.

'So, you're my little cousin. You should have seen your face just then.'

'Ariel?' He took a tentative step out from his hiding place.

'My dad made me come and find you. I think he was worried you might get lost or drown or something.'

Charlie thought he detected a smirk in her voice.

'It's nice to meet you,' he said, forcing himself to sound friendly. He slid down the dune towards her, but she had already turned back towards her horse.

'Come on. We need to get going. It'll be dark soon and the tide is on the turn. Jump up.'

'I'm sorry, I've never been on a horse before. I don't really know how to...'

Her expression mixed contempt and pity in equal measure. 'Well, you'd better get a move on if you're going to walk home. The tide comes in faster than you think round here.'

Charlie stared at her as she adjusted the reins. He knew from his mum that Ariel was fifteen; a little older than him, but it might have been years. She was taller for a start, and the threadbare riding jacket she wore gave her an adult air. Her dark eyes focused intently on the horse as if it were far better company than he could ever hope to be, and the arch of her eyebrows suggested a special contempt for the world around her. As she turned back to Charlie, he could see in her weary expression that she considered the presence of her cousin to be a colossal inconvenience.

'Actually,' Charlie said, 'I think I'll be just fine on my own.'

Ariel shrugged. 'Whatever. Stick to the line of the dunes and you'll find the footpath you came down on. That's assuming you are not totally incapable of retracing your own steps.'

And with that she pulled herself up into the saddle and galloped off towards the sea. Charlie watched her go and then, feeling as low as he had done all day, trudged back, following his own footprints to

Darkwater House.

It wasn't until he was in his attic room, changing out of his wet socks and clothes, that he realised he had left the metal detector in the dunes on the beach.

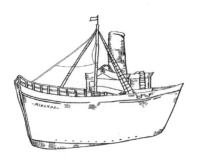

CHAPTER FOUR

'Well, this is nice!' Uncle Patrick clapped his hands. 'It's good to get the family together.'

He poured himself a generous glass of red wine and stirred the pot on the stove. The windowpane above the sink dripped with steam. 'I hope you like lentil stew, Charlie.'

'I don't think I've had it before.'

'You haven't lived. Ariel, can you clear your stuff away now, please?'

His cousin sat at the round wooden table in the centre of the kitchen, her sketch pads spread out before her like tarot cards. She was absorbed in her drawing, rubbing away with a charcoal stick and paying no attention to either her father or Charlie. Somewhere in the house a clock chimed the hour.

'Come on please, darling. You need to clear the table.'

Ariel continued sketching as Charlie peered over her shoulder.

'That's really good,' he said.

Her hand moved rapidly over the paper and the face of a beautiful young woman emerged from the page. She worked confidently, defining the bright eyes and elegant jaw line with precise strokes.

'Who is it?'

She stopped and glared at him. 'It's my mother.'

Uncle Patrick banged the oven door open and made a big show of shaking a tray of parsnips.

'Nearly done,' he said briskly. 'How about showing Charlie some of your other drawings? And then clearing up.'

Ariel scraped her chair across the flagstones and began to pack away her pad, nodding briefly at the pile of sketch books. Charlie opened the nearest one. It was filled with detailed pencil sketches of horses, trees and Ferdinand the cat.

'They're brilliant,' he said. 'I'm not good at art. I prefer football.'

Ariel's face was a mask of indifference as she packed her books.

'Some of her sketches will be on sale at our stall tomorrow,' said Uncle Patrick, a note of something between encouragement and pride in his voice. He set the pot down on the table. 'Right, Ariel, please clear these away now. They'll get food on them. And sit down, Charlie. It'll be all hands on deck tomorrow morning for the market, so I hope you're good with early starts.'

'I'm not really a morning person.' Charlie pulled his chair to the table. 'Mum says she needs a stick of dynamite to get me out of bed on school mornings rather than an alarm clock.'

'I was the same,' his uncle said, scooping a ladle full of the pale orange stew onto a plate. 'But I'm an early bird these days. I don't sleep as well as I used to.'

Charlie poked tentatively at his food with a fork. There were definitely some carrots involved in there and possibly some leeks too, but it tasted better than it looked and he was surprised at how hungry he felt. Ariel pushed her supper around her plate, an expression of extreme boredom etched on her face while her father overcompensated with a series of questions about Charlie's family and suggesting Ariel give Charlie a tour of Dunstrand the next day. She rolled her eyes.

'Do you go to a lot of these markets?' Charlie

asked, changing the subject.

'I'm trying to.'

Ariel smirked. 'It used to be all about the art for Dad,' she said. 'Now it's about the money.'

'Someone has to feed us.' There was a strained quality to Patrick's voice, as if he was trying to control his temper. 'All this has to be paid for somehow.'

'You should have thought about that before you moved us back here.'

Uncle Patrick smashed his fist down on the table making the plates jump.

'That's enough!'

His eyes were wild as he stared at his daughter, who sat there innocently turning over her food with a fork.

'It's high time you showed some respect, young lady! Especially when we have a guest.'

'It wasn't my idea to invite him here,' Ariel murmured.

'What did you say?' Her father's knuckles were white as he gripped the edge of the table.

It was Ariel's turn to be angry now. She flung her fork down on the plate and turned in fury on her father.

'Why don't you leave me alone?' she shouted.

'You're always on my case. And this is all your fault.' She flung her arms wide, taking in Charlie and everything in the room around. 'All of it!'

She kicked back her chair, which clattered onto the floor, and swept out, banging the door behind her.

Silence fell over the table and Charlie lowered his eyes to his plate, unsure what to do or say next. Quietly, he finished his meal. When he looked up, he saw his uncle opposite him sitting with his face buried in his hands. Charlie got up slowly and cleared his plate from the table, leaving it beside the sink. His uncle did not move.

Later, in the cold bathroom brushing his teeth, Charlie still felt the shock of what he had witnessed. He argued with his parents from time to time, but never like that. It was unsettling to experience that level of raw emotion up close. The wind whined round the frosted window above the sink and he spat out his toothpaste, watching it swill away down the plughole. He thought of the wide empty beach out there in the darkness and longed for London.

And what had Ariel meant? *It wasn't my idea to invite him... This is all your fault...* Maybe it wasn't just his mother's plan to pack him off here for the holidays? Uncle Patrick had wanted it too. And what could Charlie have possibly done to offend his cousin so much? She'd been sullen right from the start, spiteful even, trying to scare him down on the beach. He had done nothing to provoke her, he was certain.

He made his way along the passage to his bedroom, attuned to every unfamiliar creak and click of the house. He distracted himself by unpacking some of the football magazines he had stuffed into his case at home that morning, scattering them over the bed in order to choose one to read. But as he was sifting through them, he slowly became aware of a faint rustling sound, soft and intermittent, like someone dragging a blanket over a stone floor. He went to the window and peered out in the dark. He could see nothing but the shifting treetops. Dropping to his knees, he looked under the bed, fearful of glimpsing a mouse dart across the floor, but everything was as he had left it before supper: damp clothes flung down in a pile, jacket hanging on the hook on the back of the door... Then he noticed it: his jacket was swaying ever so slightly on its hook, the fabric gently rubbing against the woodwork; back and forth, back and forth...

He bit his lip. There was probably a draught

blowing through a crack somewhere. Carefully, and with his breath coming strangely fast and loud, he lifted the jacket down and was instantly struck by the weight in one pocket.

The brass box from the beach.

He'd forgotten all about it. He pulled it out and for a split second he thought he felt it vibrate slightly in his hand. Quickly, he stuffed it into his jacket pocket and threw it all into the wardrobe. There was a loud knock on the door behind him.

'Sorry to disturb you.' Uncle Patrick stood rubbing his hands awkwardly on the threshold. 'I wanted to apologise for earlier. Are you all right?'

Charlie composed himself. 'I'm fine. Just a bit tired from the journey. And please don't worry about this evening. I've seen Mum lose it much worse than that.'

'So have I.' Uncle Patrick smiled weakly. 'I'm glad you're OK.'

'Really. It's nothing.'

'Look. There are a few things you should know. I probably should have explained more about them earlier...'

Charlie felt his own discomfort draining away; he suddenly felt sorry for his uncle. The energetic, jovial man who had picked him up at the station had been replaced by this anxious and deflated figure, shuffling uncomfortably in the doorway. He knew he should say something but he could not find the words; then he realised that he did not need to say anything at all. He just needed to listen.

Uncle Patrick hesitated for a second. 'I've an idea,' he said. 'How's your head for heights?'

He led the way along the passage and using a pole that had been resting on top of a bookcase, flicked open a hatch in the ceiling and pulled down a folding ladder. Charlie followed his uncle up the steps. A single electric bulb hung dimly from the rafters, illuminating stacks of cardboard boxes and thick dust under the beams. Crouching low, his uncle shuffled towards a circular window at the far end of the attic.

'This is the tricky bit. Make sure you hold on to the frame.'

His uncle squeezed through the window and out onto an iron balcony, hemmed in by the slanting roof on one side and a brick chimney on the other. Gingerly, Charlie followed.

'Welcome to my secret rooftop hideout.' Some of his uncle's earlier enthusiasm was already creeping back.

Charlie gripped the rail in front of him. Below, in the moonlight, he could see the lawn and the outbuildings and the path to the beach.

'The best view is that way.' His uncle pointed upwards.

Charlie followed his finger and gasped.

The sky was alive with thousands of brilliant white stars, shimmering in the wind.

'I bet they don't look like that in London.' Uncle Patrick lit a cigarette and the tip glowed orange. That's the Plough, and you see that sort of white dusting over there? That's the Milky Way.'

'How come you know so much about the stars?'

'I got into astronomy in India. Marianne and I used to have this big old telescope and we'd set it up in the evening on the shore. The skies were so dark out there. Incredible. I like to come up here at night sometimes and look at them.'

'Marianne was my aunt wasn't she? The lady Ariel was sketching before dinner? I wish I could remember her.' The words came more easily than he had imagined. Perhaps it was the cover of darkness or the fact that there was no need to look one another in the eye.

'Yes, she was.'

Charlie waited, still looking up at the stars and listening to the wind moving through trees. After a moment his uncle began to speak again.

'I don't know how much your mum has told you, but Marianne and I met at art school when I was studying in Paris. We both wanted to see the world and so while your mum was being sensible getting qualified as a doctor, we were off travelling in Asia. It was a very simple life but we loved it. Ariel was born back here in Europe, but we both had the urge to go travelling again as a family. Your mum thought we were mad. We ended up living in India. A proper piece of paradise. I was painting and selling the odd piece to some of the tourists who passed through. There was an international college not far from us where Marianne would sometimes teach and Ariel went to school, but your cousin basically grew up outdoors, playing in the sea and on the beach. Life was pretty much perfect.'

He threw down his cigarette and flicked it with his foot to join the others in the gutter.

'One day, a few months after Ariel's thirteenth birthday, I had to go away to the city to get some paints and supplies I needed. Marianne wanted to come, but I insisted she stayed behind with Ariel. To be honest, I used to like those occasional overnight trips away. It was refreshing, but I was always glad to get back. So I left them both and took the train.'

He stopped and wiped the back of his hand across his eye.

'It's cold up here tonight.' His laugh sounded hollow.

'What happened next?' Charlie said, his gaze set firmly on the stars.

'Nobody knows exactly. They think it might have been a cobra. It must have got into the house during the night. When Ariel woke up the next morning and went in to see her mother, Marianne was already dead.' He exhaled deeply and leaned back against the chimney breast. 'You don't get paradise without the serpent. I'll never forgive myself, Charlie, as long as I live.'

'But it wasn't your fault.'

'I should have been there. Ariel thinks I should have been there. She blames me for going away that day.'

Charlie stared up at the sky. He'd never heard an adult talk like this and he was glad it was dark.

'Nothing was ever the same after that.' Uncle Patrick's voice was flat. 'We stayed out there for another year or so, but it was like the spell had been broken and there was nothing I could do to put things back to how they were before. Grief is so hard, Charlie. For a child and for an adult. I don't think it ever stops. Eventually it seemed to make more and more sense to come back to England. It's funny how strong a pull home has, even when you've been away for years. And then there were the schools and the need to actually start earning a proper living...' His voice fell away.

'And Ariel doesn't like how life is now?'

'Hates it. Resents it all. If she had her way she'd still be running barefoot beside the Indian Ocean. She blames me for bringing her back, she blames me for what happened to her mother, she blames me for trying to make a business out of my art. You saw what happened over dinner tonight. It's been like it for months and months. But you have to understand, Charlie, that your cousin has been through a lot and she doesn't really have anyone to share it all with.'

'Which was why you thought it would be a good idea to have me around here for some of the Christmas holidays.'

Uncle Patrick grimaced. 'Was it that obvious?'

'Mum must have been delighted. You've helped her out when her shifts got changed and she got to stop me chilling at home over the holidays. She doesn't really understand about...relaxing.'

'She never did.'

They both smiled.

'We should head back in,' said Uncle Patrick. 'It's getting late. I'm sorry for droning on, but it's good to have someone to talk to. It can get pretty lonely out here sometimes.'

At that moment something caught Charlie's eye. Someone was striding purposefully across the lawn wrapped in a long coat, a ring of torchlight in front and a trail of damp footprints behind. The figure wore a hood against the wind, like a monk hurrying to prayers. Uncle Patrick had noticed too. He leaned over the balcony, his eyes following closely until the figure vanished down the track to the sea.

'Ariel,' he muttered. 'She sometimes walks at night. Out for hours, on the beach and in the woods. Sometimes over to the farm. She seems to get on with Clara Cooper up there, which is something, I suppose.'

'Why's she out so late?'

'Can't sleep. Too many bad dreams. I've tried to stop her going out, but... Well you've seen how determined she can be.'

Charlie looked down at the path and tried to imagine picking his way along it in the dark with the branches pulling at him like fingers, the hedgerows alive with scurrying creatures.

'It's getting cold out here,' he said, 'and I think I need to get to bed soon.'

'Of course. Let's get back inside. And I'm sorry again about this evening.'

Alone in his room once more, Charlie pulled the covers tight and started to flick through his football magazines. Their familiarity helped keep the strangeness of his surroundings at bay and he was relieved when his eyes felt heavy. If he fell asleep quickly, it would soon be tomorrow. One day closer to Christmas; one day closer to going home.

He turned off the lamp and the window became a pale square of moonlight behind the thin curtains. Closing his eyes, he imagined his own bedroom, plotting out in his mind where everything stood, willing away the walls of Darkwater House and listening for the trains. Just once, he thought he heard a brief, soft rustling coming from inside the wardrobe, but a wave of deep fatigue was already rolling over him, pulling him down into heavy sleep.

CHAPTER FIVE

It was still dark when the Land Rover approached Dunstrand. Charlie, wedged in the back seat between packed boxes of china mugs, felt frozen and only half-awake. Ariel was in the front next to her father, balancing two boxes on her knee. Every now and then Charlie caught a glimpse of their faces bathed in the feeble glow of the dashboard lights. Nobody spoke.

Despite the early hour, the market square was ablaze when they arrived, filled with people bustling back and forth in the bitter cold, setting out trestle tables under coloured canvas roofs.

'The Christmas Market goes back to medieval times,' Uncle Patrick said, slamming the door. 'There'll be people from all over the county here today.'

Ariel yawned.

Beneath electric lights and clouds of breath, the

stall holders were unpacking their wares. The three of them found their own pitch between a smiling lady selling homemade jewellery and a man swathed in an enormous striped scarf, who was unloading Christmas decorations from the back of a van.

'I'll set the pictures out,' Ariel said, in a tone that did not invite discussion.

'Let me get the easels up first,' her father said. 'Charlie, can you go and get me a cup of coffee? There's a van on the corner. Get something for you two as well.'

Charlie wandered off in the direction his uncle indicated, squeezing between the narrow aisles of the market stalls. One was already set out with a catch of fish, their rainbow scales gleaming on packed ice. Another was festooned with pheasants and rabbits on hooks; a third crammed with multi-coloured jars of sweets. The smells of fresh-baked bread and petrol from the generators mingled in the air.

Charlie returned with coffee and two cups of hot chocolate to find Ariel engrossed in hanging pictures on a cork-board. There were several watercolours of the beach and the lighthouse. One or two were charcoal sketches of horses.

'Are those yours?' Charlie asked.

She nodded.

'I really like them. I hope they sell.'

She shrugged. 'Don't care if they do or don't.'

There were dark circles under her eyes.

A noisy group of farmers in waxed jackets and flat hats had gathered outside the Mariner's Arms pub on the corner and were swapping jokes and laughing while the landlord toiled away behind a giant gas barbecue. According to the chalkboard on the wall, there would soon be bacon rolls and sausages for breakfast.

'Have you ever thought of opening a shop?' Charlie asked, as his uncle set out the reindeer mugs on the stall.

'I'd love to. But I need to get better known in the area. More established.'

'You need a proper website,' Ariel observed.

'I look forward to you designing it for me. Now, are we all set?'

They were busy all morning with a steady stream of customers. Charlie found he enjoyed working the stall, taking the money and serving people while Ariel did the gift-wrapping with speed and skill. Uncle Patrick chatted to the customers, explaining more about the pictures, gently cajoling them towards a sale. For most of the time, Ariel said very little. She became animated only once, when a tall lady in a thick fake-fur jacket glided like a dancer through the crowds towards them. She wore square, black-framed glasses with long greying hair spilling out from under a bobble hat.

'Ariel! What are you doing here?'

'Hello, Miss Stanford. I'm just helping out my dad.'

'Ah yes, of course. I should have known he would have a stall here today. Where is he?'

'He's gone to get some lunch.'

A brief look of disappointment flickered over Miss Stanford's face. 'Never mind. I'm sure I'll bump into him later. And I hope you're not going to be too busy to help out this week? There's still a lot of painting to be done before the performance.'

'I'll be there tomorrow, don't worry.'

'And who's this?'

'I'm Charlie. Ariel's cousin.'

'Miss Stanford. Pleased to meet you. I teach at the school and also run the children's music group in Dunstrand. You're welcome to come and see the performance if you're staying with us long enough.'

'Thank you,' said Charlie.

'Well, have a good day both of you – and Ariel, do

tell your father I was asking after him.'

She moved away, her bobble hat visible among the crowd until she turned the corner by the pub and disappeared.

'She seems nice,' Charlie said.

'The only decent teacher at the school. The rest are useless.'

When Uncle Patrick returned with a sandwich a little while later, he insisted the children take a lunch break too; Charlie suspected another ruse to force them together. In silence, they trudged round the market, stopping at the pub where someone had set up a pen with two reindeer. A little crowd had gathered, taking selfies. Instinctively, Charlie hung back while his cousin patted the animals over the bars of the pen.

'I think I'll stay here for a while,' she told him. 'You go and find some food if you want to. I'm not that hungry.'

Charlie was silent for a moment. Then he said: 'Ariel, what's the problem?'

She looked at him with wide-eyed innocence. 'What do you mean?'

'I mean since I arrived, you've tried to run me down on your horse, have barely spoken two words to me and now you're abandoning me in the middle of the market. What's your problem?'

'Abandoning you? Can't you cope on your own for half an hour?' Her voice was soaked in sarcasm.

'Look,' Charlie felt his temper rising, 'if it makes any difference to you, it wasn't my idea to come here. Believe me, there are plenty of other things I'd rather be doing than spending a week stuck in the middle of nowhere with you.'

His words hung in the cold air and they glared at one another.

'Well, if that's how you feel,' she said, 'I would have thought you'd be glad to be on your own for a bit.'

And with that she marched off.

Charlie kicked the cobbles in frustration. Somehow, she'd made it seem as if it was all his fault. Ridiculous! Well, he wasn't going to go begging. If she wanted a week of low-level hostility, she was welcome to it. There was no helping some people. The barbecue grill was still sizzling away near the pub door and he gazed at the menu. Maybe some lunch would take his mind off it all. The steak sandwich looked good, but then he realised with annoyance that he had already spent most of the money his mum had given him in the blowout on the train. He settled for a single hotdog, taking savage mouthfuls as he wandered down a side street towards the sea.

He soon found himself by a little harbour where a handful of boats rocked on the rising tide. A tiny parade of shops faced the water, one of which had 'Cartwright's Antiques: Buying, Selling & Free Valuations' stencilled in black letters on the glass. Its window was crammed with peculiar trinkets laid out on a strip of red velvet: silver spoons with ornately carved handles, military medals and a teddy bear so old you could see the stuffing through the worn patches of its fur. Charlie thought suddenly of his find on the beach and plunged his hand inside his coat pocket. Yes, there it was. He pushed open the shop door and went inside.

He found himself in a low-ceilinged room, piled high with antiques. Dark wooden tables were stacked with china dishes which rose in miniature towers between polished copper pans, silver clocks and a plaster bust of a Roman emperor. Through a low doorway ahead, Charlie could see a woman with skin the colour of the porcelain plates around her. She was examining a gold bracelet through an eyeglass, and a young man in a corduroy jacket leaned forward over the counter, anxiously awaiting her verdict. At the far end of the room was a door with the words 'Arnold Cartwright's Office' printed on it in large capital letters. The door was slightly ajar. Through it, Charlie could hear the voice of a man on the telephone.

'I want all the lists,' he was saying in a breathy, impatient tone. 'As soon as you 'ave 'em... No. Can't wait till New Year... I'm not 'aving anyone else stealin' a march on those 'ouse clearances... Yes, I know they mostly turn up junk, but occasionally there's something worth 'avin'... Remember that Constable they found in that rectory a few years back? That's what I mean... Mind you keep on your toes.'

There was the sound of a receiver being banged down.

'Miss Timms,' the voice shouted, 'Where are you?'

Instinctively, Charlie stepped back to conceal himself in an alcove beside a polished suit of armour: it wasn't his fault the office door had been left open, but he had no desire to be accused of eavesdropping.

The man who emerged bore a striking resemblance to a well-fed pig. His head was round, pink and bald except for some straggling blond hair over his ears and collar. His pale eyes blinked out above a pair of half-glasses which rested on the wide snout of his nose. He wore a tweed suit with a red waistcoat that strained over his belly as he shuffled past. Charlie would not have been surprised to see a curly tail protruding from the back of his trousers as he went by.

'Miss Timms, are you deaf?'

'I'm with a customer, Mr Cartwright,' said the lady behind the counter.

From his hiding place, Charlie saw the man's scowl melt into an ingratiating smile.

'Oh, I didn't realise. Do carry on. I'll be back when you're done.'

'Yes, Mr Cartwright.'

Charlie pressed himself deeper into the shadows and watched Cartwright retreat to his office. The woman at the counter was now in animated conversation with her customer about the potential value of the bracelet, so Charlie hung back, idly pulling the brass box from his pocket and examining it once more. What if it really was valuable? Could he sell it and keep the money? He didn't see why not. He'd found it, fair and square.

All of a sudden, someone seized him by the wrist and demanded: 'Where did you get that?'

Charlie gasped and looked up to see an old man holding him in a grip of surprising strength. His bright eyes blazed with a fierce intensity and it took Charlie a moment to realise that he must have been lurking nearby all along, obscured by the gloom of the shop. His hair was white and close-cropped, while the beard beneath curled thickly about his cheeks and chin. His overcoat looked expensive and he wore an immaculate red silk tie and white shirt. The whole effect was of a sinister Santa Claus materialising from among the bric-à-brac.

'Get off me or I'll call the police,' Charlie stammered.

The man blinked twice and released his grip.

'Forgive me. I was forgetting myself,' the voice was well-mannered and apologetic. 'I did not mean to alarm you.'

Charlie took a pace back.

'Tell me, young man, where did you get that box?'

'I found it on the beach.'

The man looked Charlie up and down as if trying to decide whether he was telling the truth.

'When did you find it?'

'Yesterday. Buried in the sand. I didn't steal it, if that's what you're thinking.'

The man seemed satisfied. 'Oh, I'm sure you're an honest lad. But listen.' He leaned forward so close that Charlie could see the individual hairs in his beard.

'If you have any sense, you'll take this box out of this shop right now and throw it back into the sea where it belongs. Drown it. Deep water, mind you. The deepest you can find. And then forget all about it.'

'Why?'

'Because that box is dangerous. Extremely dangerous.'

The man stared at him intently, as if forcing his words into Charlie's brain, then threw up his hands, palms outstretched. 'But it's up to you. You found it. It's yours now. But remember this, young man: they call them the ghost tides round here. Big winter storms that unearth things that were buried long ago. Things that are best left undisturbed.'

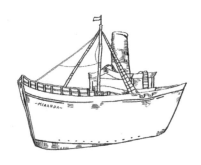

CHAPTER SIX

'Is everything all right here?'

It took Charlie a moment to realise the young woman from behind the counter was now standing beside them. Her eyes travelled slowly between him and the old man, trying to work out if they knew one another or if some sort of unexpected violence was about to burst out and shatter the afternoon. The man's gaze drilled into Charlie for a second longer.

'Is everything all right, sir?' she repeated.

Now it was the old man's turn to notice her presence. 'All right? I suspect that very much depends on our young friend here. It's in his hands now.' And without saying another word, he turned and left the shop.

Charlie's heart was pounding fast. It had all happened so quickly and been so...bizarre.

'Well, can I help you, young man? Were you

looking for anything in particular?'

Charlie composed himself and looked down at the box in his hands. 'Yes. This. Your sign says you do free valuations, so I wondered if you could tell me what it's worth, please.'

'Follow me.'

At the counter, she examined the box under a bright light, holding it carefully in her delicate hands.

'Well, this is unusual. May I ask where it comes from?'

Charlie explained.

'Buried treasure?' She raised her eyebrows. 'Now that's not something we get in here every day.'

At that moment, the owner of the shop came shuffling out of his office. He pushed past Miss Timms and thrust his face in front of the box like a hungry pig at a trough.

'What 'ave you got there? Looks an odd 'un.'

'It's quite old.' Miss Timms had her eyeglass back in. 'This tree trunk carved into the top looks very unusual. And then these words: *All the devils are here.*' Very peculiar. The catch is seized up, but it's well preserved, given that it has probably been in the sea for so long.'

'You found it in the sea?' Cartwright seemed to

have been struck by a bolt of electricity. 'Where?'

'Over by the Serpent's Tongue,' said Charlie slowly. He could see a speck of excitement dancing in Cartwright's eyes which made him uneasy.

Cartwright grabbed the box and lifted it closer to his face. A slow grin broke over his lips, exposing a line of yellowing teeth. Then, as if catching himself, his mouth dropped and he was business-like once more.

'Well, all very interestin' young man. But I'm sorry to disappoint you if you've been dreamin' of striking it rich. My view is that, while this is certainly a curiosity, it's no more than a trinket. No real value at all.'

Miss Timms opened her mouth as if to say something, but her boss laid a fat hand on her arm. 'Please could you go into my office for a moment, Miss Timms? I can't get the lid off the fish food.' He waved his fingers at Charlie by way of explanation. 'Touch of arthritis, you see.'

Reluctantly, Miss Timms left them and Cartwright peered at Charlie over his glasses.

'What did you say your name was, lad?'

'Charlie Mills.'

'Now then, Charlie, as I was sayin', this box is

unusual, but I doubt it's anything special. All sorts of stuff gets washed up round 'ere. Big tides you see, especially in winter. Every few years we get a really big one. A ghost tide; 'ad one only the other week. Always sets off the more superstitious folk round 'ere, but that's another story. You did the right thing by bringin' it in for me to look at and I wouldn't want that initiative to go…unrewarded.' He licked his lips. 'I'll give you ten pounds for it. That's probably a little on the generous side, but it is nearly Christmas.'

Charlie stared into the round pink face and the watery eyes.

'No,' he said and reached over the counter to take the box back.

Arnold Cartwright's hands slapped down on his wrists. 'Twenty.'

Charlie shook his head.

'Twenty-five. It's my final offer. Think of all the sweets you could buy with that!'

Charlie shook himself free and pulled the box over the counter. 'Please don't take me for an idiot, Mr Cartwright. You tell me it's worth nothing and yet in the space of ten seconds you've more than doubled your first offer. That tells me I'm better to hold on to it for now. Merry Christmas.'

Charlie strode towards the shop door and behind him he heard Cartwright swear viciously under his breath. Outside in the cold afternoon air, Charlie hurried back towards the market square, pausing once to look over his shoulder. For a second, he thought he glimpsed a stout figure following behind him, but then it scuttled into a doorway and vanished from his sight.

CHAPTER SEVEN

Charlie couldn't sleep that night. Darkwater House was in a restless mood, full of creaks and ticks as if it too was unable to settle. He must have dozed off at one point but found himself switching from one side of the bed to the other between shallow dreams and noisy springs.

He sat up and switched on the light.

His phone told him it was half past midnight. The same anxious mix of isolation, fatigue and homesickness that had struck him when he first arrived began to churn inside him once more. He rolled out of bed and pulled on his sweatshirt. He shook himself and stretched, trying to release the tension from his limbs and mind. He rubbed at the bruise on his arm. At least it was fading now, but the memory of how it had happened was still vivid. He thought back to school and the playground and the incident began to run like a film in his head, blotting out, for a few moments at least, the strangeness of his current surroundings.

Joe Dixon and his gang in the year above had had it in for him and Sanjay since the start of term. For some reason Joe thought them easy targets for the sort of low-level, idiotic stuff that bullies seem to delight in: a shove in the back in the lunch queue; a trip in the corridor; a passing punch at the bus stop; and all of it exhausting and dispiriting. The gnawing anxiety that Joe and his mates might be there at the school gate or in the same carriage on the tube on the way home had been a constant backdrop to the term.

This particular incident had happened when Charlie was playing football with Sanjay. They were using the new ball Charlie's dad had given him before he went off on his latest trip. Joe and two of his mates had been circling the playground like vultures for a while and they were clearly at a loose end: a recipe for trouble. Sanjay had spotted the danger straight away but Charlie was defiant. What right did fatheads like Joe Dixon have to spoil their game? They should just carry on, even though he could feel the fun draining out of their kick-about like water from a bath.

In the end, Sanjay stopped playing. 'Come on.

Let's go. Joe nicked my trainers out of my bag last week. I can't prove it but I'm sure it was him. My mum went mad at me for losing them. Best keep clear. Bunch of idiots, all of them.'

But by then it was too late.

Joe was swaggering directly towards them, stocky and strong. There was a big gap between his front teeth.

'Let us play,' he grinned. It wasn't a request.

'Sorry, we've just finished,' Charlie had said, looking up at him and clutching the ball tightly to his chest.

'But we want to play.'

It was then that Joe unleashed the punch. Charlie half turned and it caught him flush on the arm. He dropped the ball and in an instant one of the gang had kicked it across the playground. Joe laughed. 'I knew you'd let us play in the end.'

Charlie had come home without his ball that day and now, as he looked around the unfamiliar room, he felt the pain of the incident all over again. Suddenly he was annoyed with himself for letting the whole thing get to him once more, resentful that the reach of those bullies could touch him even in this faraway place.

He took a sip of water from the glass on the bedside table. The wind had dropped and he could hear the distant break of the sea.

The box sat on the windowsill, flush against the frame. He stared at it. Why had the old man said it was dangerous? It looked harmless enough. But there had been something in the urgency of his voice... *Drown it...* Charlie began to feel foolish. This was the stuff of fairy tales, the kind of thing he and Sanjay would have laughed at back in London. And yet somehow here, in this place... He looked at the figure carved into the lid, trapped inside its tree-trunk prison. His mouth felt dry.

His water glass was empty. Reluctantly, he decided he would have to refill it. Using the torch on his phone to light the way, he made his way to the bathroom at the end of the corridor. Ariel and Uncle Patrick's rooms were at the front of the house, so there was little chance of disturbing them, and he moved swiftly, not allowing his imagination to roam. But on his way back, something stopped him dead in his tracks, chilling his skin.

It was the sound of a child's voice, singing quietly in the darkness.

'Ring a-ring-a roses... A pocket full of posies...'

The voice sounded like it belonged to a little girl. It was soft and coming from behind the same bedroom door as before.

'Atishoo, Atishoo, we all fall down...'

The singing stopped.

Charlie held his breath, listening. In his head he knew he should now throw open that bedroom door, switch on all the lights and search the room. But he was also certain he would find nothing there. Instead he ran: back along the corridor, pulling his door shut and jumping into bed to wrap the blankets around him as quickly as he could.

His breath came fast. That was twice he had heard it now. Maybe he was coming down with something? Or was the whole freakish nature of this place getting to him? Or could it be Ariel? His fear began to ebb away; that would explain it! It was a girl's voice, and Ariel was the only girl at Darkwater House. And she was odd, let's face it, and clearly unhappy with him being here. This would be just her idea of winding him up, like she had done with the horse on the beach. She was even wandering round the garden late last night, so it was quite probable she was still awake now, trying to make him feel uncomfortable and unwelcome. It was clearly some sort of trick, a recording or something. It would be easy enough to do if you knew the house well. When the time was right, he'd have it out with her. He wasn't playing this game.

Calmer now, Charlie rolled over and reached out to turn off the light. But as he did so, for the second time that night, he froze with shock.

The box was no longer on the windowsill where he had left it.

Instead, it was sitting on the floor at the foot of his bed. Slowly, he crawled over the sheets towards it and leaned down to pick it up. It twitched in his hands as if it were alive.

Charlie yelped and dropped the box, which went tumbling across the floor. He stared at it for a second, then grabbed a spare blanket. Wrapping the box tightly inside it, he stuffed it into the furthest reaches of the wardrobe. Next he slammed the door shut and turned the key. Then, for good measure, he dragged a chair against the wardrobe and wedged it tight under the handle.

Tomorrow, he resolved, he would follow the old man's advice and throw the box back into the sea.

CHAPTER EIGHT

Uncle Patrick was pouring tea at the kitchen table when Charlie came down for breakfast. Ariel was sitting opposite him, dressed head to toe in black, reading a book.

'Good Morning! Sleep well?'

Charlie now recognised the note of excessive cheeriness in his uncle's voice as a way of compensating for the silence of his daughter. 'OK,' he said, 'but I got woken up by some noises in the night.'

He studied his cousin for a tell-tale sign, but Ariel merely turned a page with exaggerated indifference.

'Well, it's an old house,' said Uncle Patrick, 'and it does makes some peculiar sounds from time to time. There's the odd mouse around too, I'm afraid. Might well have been one of them. There's muesli in the cupboard and I can probably squeeze another cup out of this if you'd like.' He waved the pot in the air.

Studying his cousin over the rim of his tea mug, Charlie considered asking her outright, there and then, about the singing he had heard in the night. But watching his uncle bustle around the kitchen, trying so hard to keep things normal, he realised this was neither the time nor the place. It would only hurt his uncle to see the cousins arguing. No, this was something that needed to be sorted out away from adult interference. He would have to be patient and choose his moment. He also needed to engineer an escape from them both at some point so he could get rid of that damned box. The day seemed filled with problems. He chewed his cereal but didn't have much appetite.

'Now then, Ariel,' Uncle Patrick said, 'I've got to do a stock-take after yesterday. What have you two got planned for the day?'

There was no way for Ariel to avoid such a direct question, and Charlie resisted the urge to fill the silence out of politeness. Slowly, Ariel put down her book.

'I thought I might go for a ride over the headland.'

'Well that's not very good for Charlie, is it, darling? You know he doesn't ride.'

She shrugged. 'That's not my problem.'

So that's how it's going to be, thought Charlie. They had managed an uneasy truce on the way back from the market yesterday, but the atmosphere between them remained as frosty as the weather.

'Well there is something you can both help me with,' Uncle Patrick said hurriedly. 'We haven't got a Christmas tree yet, but I saw David Cooper at the market yesterday and he said we can take one from that little copse of his in the top field. Why don't you go up to the farm this morning and cut us a tree?'

There was something so desperate about his uncle's desire for the cousins to get along that Charlie could only agree.

'Sounds good,' he said, trying to look cheerful. The suggestion also had the distinct attraction of getting him out of the house.

'We'll have to be back by midday,' Ariel said, getting to her feet. 'I've promised Miss Stanford I'll finish painting the set for the Christmas concert.'

'How is Sarah? I was sorry to miss her yesterday.'

'She's fine.'

'I painted the set for my school play last term,' Charlie chimed in. 'Perhaps I can help out too?'

Uncle Patrick clapped his hands. 'Excellent! I

knew you two would find plenty in common once you tried.'

Ariel fired him a look that was both patronising and pitying.

'I'll see you round the front in five minutes,' she told Charlie. 'Don't be late or I'll go without you.'

CHAPTER NINE

It had frozen overnight and the puddles on the track up to the farm were thick with ice. They made their way along the path in silence between hedgerows of tangled brown twigs and green ivy, dusted in the hollows with sparkling frost. They walked with their backs to the sea, away from the beach and the lighthouse, inland under a watery sun. The cold seeped in through Charlie's wellington boots and he wriggled his toes to keep them warm, unwilling to acknowledge any discomfort to his cousin.

'How far is it?' he asked.

'Half a mile. We should call in at the farm first and let them know.'

Around the corner, a line of wood smoke rose from a squat brick house, sheltered by the gentle curve of the hill. As they drew closer, Charlie could see a small farmyard bordered by a long, low barn.

The noise and smell of cows hung in the cold air.

'They're finishing milking,' said Ariel, swinging her legs easily over the gate. 'I hope cows don't freak you out too.'

Charlie pretended not to hear and clambered after her into the yard; immediately a furious barking began and a black terrier came speeding round the farmhouse wall. It jumped up at Ariel, who rubbed its head vigorously, and between excited yelps it licked her hand with a pink tongue. Charlie shrank back but was determined not to let his discomfort show, even as the dog turned its attention to him and began to paw at his legs. He fixed a grin on his face and waited for it to stop.

'Get down!'

A voice bellowed across the yard and instantly the dog slunk away towards the farmhouse door. A man in blue overalls and a grey flat cap was standing outside the milking parlour. His face looked too old for his body, his features scoured like a weathered statue, but he moved like a young man when he came striding lightly across the yard. 'Morning, Ariel. Who's your friend?'

Charlie explained, keeping a careful eye on the dog.

'He won't hurt you, lad,' the man said. 'I'm David

Cooper. Welcome to the farm.'

'We've come to get the tree,' said Ariel.

'Yes, I mentioned it to your dad yesterday. Top field, you know the one.'

Two small children appeared at a first-floor window of the farmhouse, standing on the window ledge, waving and giggling. Ariel waved back.

'Rose! William! Get down from there!' David shook his head in disapproval. 'They're going wild waiting for Christmas. I should pen them up with the pigs.'

The children scrambled from view, laughing hysterically.

'Why don't you pop into the parlour and say hello to Clara while I go and find the axe for you?' David looked at Charlie with a twinkle in his eye. 'My mother still likes to sit in on milking every now and then – just to make sure I don't make a mess of it.'

The parlour was dim and smelled of warm straw and dung. Two rows of black-and-white cows stood peacefully between metal rails on either side of a central aisle, while the hum and clack of the milking machine beat out a steady rhythm that echoed back off the walls. Charlie screwed up his nose and followed his cousin to the far wall where a wicker chair had been set on a raised concrete platform. There sat a white-haired old lady with her eyes closed, her head rocking gently back and forth in time with the milking machine. She was wrapped in a thick blanket and shawl and there was a sleepy Labrador curled up at her feet. It raised an ear and opened an eye as they approached.

'Is that you, Ariel?' The old lady stirred in her chair.

'Hello, Clara.' Ariel's voice had a warmth he had not heard before. 'How are you?'

'Getting older and slower, older and slower. Is that someone with you?'

'Yes, my cousin, Charlie. He's going home in a few days.'

'Come here, Charlie,' the old lady's voice was quiet but clear. 'That's it. Don't mind Pebble.'

Charlie approached, looking warily at the dog which was now sitting up on its front paws. Then the old lady did something Charlie was not expecting. She reached forward and grasped his face, running her leathery fingers over his cheeks, nose and brow. It was only when he looked back into the wrinkled face and opaque eyes that he realised she was blind.

'You are a handsome boy,' she smiled. 'And how

are you enjoying yourself so far?'

'It's a bit of a change from London.'

'I'm certain it is. I do hope you will be here for the Christmas concert. My grandchildren William and Rose have been practising their songs all week.' She took Ariel's hand. 'Miss Stanford is doing such good things here for the children. And so are you, my dear.'

Charlie saw his cousin's eyes soften.

'Nobody else thinks so,' she said quietly.

Clara stroked her face tenderly. 'You see the world differently, my dear Ariel. You perceive things that others do not. You hear things others do not and that is a gift as well as a burden, as you and I have discussed many times.'

Charlie was about to say something, but just then David Cooper emerged from among the cows, a long-handled axe over his shoulder. 'Here you go. Be careful with it. I don't mind you chopping your arms off, just don't blunt the blade.'

He rested it against the wall and turned back out into the yard, but as Charlie went to follow, Clara reached out again and pulled him towards her. She ran her hands over his face once more as if she were following a line of braille. Charlie was seized by an unnerving sensation that she was trying to read his thoughts.

'I'm very pleased to have met you, young man. I think you may sense more of the world than you realise. Far more. Your cousin can and does; I suspect you do too, if you listen carefully enough.'

Charlie mumbled something incomprehensible, conscious that Ariel was watching them both intently.

Clara's eyes were moist and milky white. 'Look after one another,' she said, squeezing his hand with surprising force. 'Listen for the echoes in the shadows – and take great care.'

She released her grip and they left her to settle back into her chair, her eyes closed once again, humming gently, listening to the familiar sounds of the herd.

Out in the sunlight, they joined the track once more. After a few hundred yards it became a bridleway, winding up the gentle slope to the top field. The sun had touched one side of the verge now and the frost was shrinking back where the light fell. The axe sat heavy on Charlie's shoulder. Eventually they reached a wooden gate which opened out into a field of rough grass. There was a small, tumbledown outhouse in one corner with an iron drinking trough beside it and a wire fence all around. The black horse, which Charlie had seen Ariel riding on the day he arrived, was grazing nearby. It lifted its head at their approach and trotted over to them, snorting hot clouds into the morning air.

Ariel kissed the horse on the forehead. 'Hello Bobby! How are you?'

'Is he yours?' Charlie asked.

'No, he belongs to the Coopers. But they let me ride him whenever I want. He roams about some of these fields and stays down in the paddock at Darkwater a lot too.' She rubbed the horse's nose and it gave a little whinny of pleasure. 'We'll be back soon, Bobby. I need you to pull the cart for us in a while.'

She set off up the field, making for a little copse of fir trees at the top where the stone wall broke and the grass was still white with frost.

Charlie hurried to keep up. 'What was that old lady talking about back there?' he asked.

Ariel said simply: 'She understands.'

'She seemed a bit weird to me. Has she got, what's it called? Dementia?'

Ariel stopped and turned on him. 'Why would you even say something like that? You don't get it, do you? Nobody round here gets it. Old people like Clara should be listened to and respected – not laughed at. You see all this? These fields, these woods, the sea? Clara's been part of this place for nearly a century. She knows everyone and everything. She feels this place, every layer of it. Not everyone who seems different is crazy, you know.'

She turned and carried on up the hill, leaving Charlie stunned by the violence of her outburst. She reached the top of the field and stalked furiously among the Christmas trees. By the time he had joined her, she had already selected one. As he caught her up, she demanded the axe. He passed it to her, and she swung it fiercely at the trunk. The blade bit into the bark, exposing the pale interior, and for a few minutes there was only the sound of distant gulls and the thwack of the blows. Finally, Ariel threw the axe down and flexed her fingers. There was a sheen of sweat on her brow.

'Your turn,' she panted.

Charlie seized the handle, keen to show he was equal to the task. It was harder work than he had imagined, and his face was red and his fingers sore by the time the tree finally fell. When it did so, he felt absurdly proud.

They stood there for a moment, catching their breath, and Charlie sensed his cousin was calmer, her anger fading. Together they dragged the Christmas tree back down to the paddock, where Ariel hitched the horse to a little wooden cart that had been tucked away inside the outhouse. Charlie helped heave the tree onto the back of the cart and then climbed up beside Ariel onto the seat at the front. Soon they were jolting back down the track towards Darkwater House.

The clip of the horse's hooves rang out against the hard ground. Ariel stared straight ahead, concentrating on the road. Charlie gripped the sides of the cart as it swayed along and suddenly he sensed the time was right.

'Ariel, have you been playing tricks on me?'

'What are you talking about?'

'Last night. I heard some weird noises in the house. I heard them when I first got here as well. It sounded like children playing. Have you been trying to scare me?'

He watched her closely: if she lied to him he was sure he would read it in her face. Her brow creased slightly and when she spoke, her voice was more gentle than usual.

'Children playing? How do you mean?'

'Singing. Laughing. But all really faint. Sounded like they might be about four or five years old. Was it you messing around? Tell me the truth.'

Ariel stopped the cart abruptly and looked at him. Her eyes were cloudy with confusion, and slowly they appeared to brighten, like the sun breaking through a cloud, and then, quite unexpectedly, her expression melted to a smile. She looked less intimidating and, feeling bolder, Charlie spoke again.

'Well? Was it you?'

'So you've been hearing voices in Darkwater House?' she said, finally.

'Yes.'

She clenched her fists and let out a sudden yell of triumph. 'I knew it!'

'Knew what?'

She seized his hands and gripped them tightly. 'Clara was right about you, Charlie. Exactly right. You can sense this stuff too.'

'What stuff?'

'I've heard those voices on and off in that house since the day we first moved in. Dad thought I was crazy when I mentioned it. He couldn't hear anything at all. In the end he got so worried that he sent me to the doctor and then a psychiatrist. None of them believed me. None of them apart from Clara.' The words were tumbling out fast now. 'But I got sick of the doctors and my dad telling me I was mad, so in the end I pretended I couldn't hear the voices at all. I told them I'd made the whole thing up just to get them off my back. But I still hear the voices in the house. Every night. I know they're real. And now you can hear them too.'

'Who are they?'

'Clara says they are the voices of ghosts, Charlie. And she used to hear them too, years ago when she was a little girl visiting the house. They are the echoes in the shadows she was talking about, part of the world that sits just beneath the surface of our own. But as she's grown older, she says she can no longer tune in and hear them. They've faded for her. But I can hear them. And it was only me who could – until you came along.'

'But who are they?'

'Two children who lived at Darkwater House centuries ago. They still play together, even though they died long ago. From time to time you catch them singing and laughing together, in the corridors or in some of the rooms in the oldest part of the house.

They were happy there.'

Charlie studied his cousin closely, half expecting her to break into a sarcastic laugh or to start mocking him for his naivety, but she was sincere, he was convinced of it. She let go of his hands. 'You are the first person I've come across who can hear the voices too.'

'You called them...ghosts,' the word sounded strange in his mouth. 'Really? And if you're right, what should we do about them?'

She considered for a moment and geed up the horse. The cart jolted and rocked down the hill. 'Nothing. They're harmless. We don't need to do anything. It's enough for me to know that I've been right all along.'

'Should we tell your dad?'

'Definitely not. He makes such a big deal of things. He'll just start raking it all up again. I'm done with doctors and shrinks.'

'I think he's worried about you. Wouldn't it help just to set things straight?'

Ariel shook her head. 'It's enough that I know.' She smiled. 'And if we get Dad involved he'll just start bothering you about it all as well and he'll think we're both crazy. I wonder why you can hear the voices like I can?'

Charlie shrugged. 'Maybe it's something in the family DNA.'

They exchanged a grin.

'I'm sorry I was mean to you when you first arrived,' she said.

'That's OK. I wasn't very happy about coming here to stay, to be honest. My mum's a pain when she gets an idea into her head. There's no shifting her.'

'Just like her brother.'

They both laughed.

Back home, they unhitched the cart and Ariel led the horse to the courtyard behind the house. Charlie kept at a watchful distance as the heavy hooves crunched over the gravel towards a stable that looked out onto a corner of a field beside the house. Inside it smelt of hay and musty sacks.

'Hold this while I brush him down,' she thrust the bridle into Charlie's hand.

He stood there uneasily, watching her work down the horse's flanks, wondering how she could be so unconcerned moving round this unpredictable mass of muscle and bone. She looked up.

'Pat him if you like. He won't bite.'

The horse's mane was like rope.

'Pass me his coat.' She nodded towards the pegs on the back wall. 'We'll keep him down here tonight. I like it when he comes to stay, and it'll be warmer here than up in the top field.'

Charlie sidled cautiously round and reached up. The coat was deep red and embroidered with intricate pictures of birds and trees. There were tiny loops of fabric with little decorations of sparkling golden thread stitched to catch the light. When he looked closer, hidden among the design, he saw small silver trinkets which looked as if they had come from a Christmas cracker.

'Did you make that?'

She nodded.

'It's really good.'

She smiled. 'Thanks. Come on. We need to be at the church hall before the rehearsal starts.'

Charlie followed her, then stopped and turned back to deliver the briefest of pats to the horse's nose.

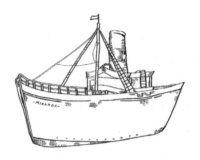

CHAPTER TEN

Miss Sarah Stanford stood on the stage with her index finger pressed to her lips. For a moment the excited chatter of the children on the floor of the hall continued unabated. Then gradually it began to subside, until everyone was standing still, looking up at her with expectant eyes. Miss Stanford pushed her glasses back onto the bridge of her nose and smiled. Her bobble hat and winter coat were draped on a chair beside her, looking as if a polar bear had come in from the cold to watch the final rehearsal of the Dunstrand Children's Christmas Concert. The performers were fizzing with excitement, the effort of staying quiet almost too much for them.

'We're going to practise our songs today,' she announced. 'Mr Brooke will play the piano and I want you to watch me, not him, as I will be conducting.'

Mr Brooke adjusted his glasses and shuffled his

sheets of music, peering at the keys intently.

'And please don't touch the set,' Miss Stanford's tone shifted to emphasise the serious nature of the instruction. 'A lot of the scenery is still wet. As you can see it is getting a final coat of paint now.'

Charlie and Ariel, dressed in baggy blue overalls, raised their brushes in acknowledgement from the back of the stage and some of the children laughed.

'Now,' Miss Stanford continued, 'I would like you all to – quietly – make your way to the centre of the stage and we will start with the first song, "We Wish You A Merry Christmas".'

The children swarmed forward in a babble of noise. Their energy was infectious and, as the first bars floated through the hall, Charlie found himself humming along with the tune. His job was the easy one. Ariel had sketched out the designs of toys, elves and giant parcels onto the scenery flats earlier in the week and had given him strict instructions for painting in the colours. He recognised two of the children from his visit to the farm: Rose and William, the Cooper grandchildren, almost identical in matching blue sweaters and pudding-bowl haircuts.

The rehearsal continued and Charlie worked methodically, occasionally glancing round at his cousin in the wings on the opposite side of the stage. Her tongue poked out as she concentrated on her work, her long black hair pulled back in a pony-tail to keep it out of the paint. She was totally immersed in her task and Charlie recognised the same intensity that he had seen in her face when she was riding her horse. He took extra care with his painting. Somehow, he didn't want to disappoint her.

Ariel looked up at him, a pencil tucked behind her right ear. 'Paint this one next when you've done that. I said I would help fix up some of the kids' costumes.'

Miss Stanford made the children run through a couple more songs, finishing with an enthusiastic version of 'Ding Dong Merrily On High' complete with ear-splitting handbell chorus, before they all scampered to the back of the hall for orange squash and biscuits. Ariel stood among the throng attempting to pin a pair of antlers to a small boy's hat. Outside, the light was beginning to fade; these were the shortest days of the year, but for the young cast, Charlie reflected, they were the longest too. Christmas crept up slowly.

Miss Stanford approached Charlie with a mug of tea.

'Thank you for volunteering,' she said. 'It means

so much to us to be able to put on a production like this.'

'Happy to help.' Charlie straightened up and stretched.

'How are you finding Dunstrand?'

'It's different from London.'

'I miss London,' Miss Stanford said wistfully. 'I used to love all the concerts and the music. So many things to be part of; so many wonderful things; so many people to meet.'

'Why did you leave?'

She smiled. 'My mother's not well. She can't really manage on her own any more so I'm back here and determined to make the best of it.'

'I'm sorry.'

She shrugged and looked towards the children running excitedly around. 'At least I have this. It makes it all worthwhile.'

At that moment, the door at the far end of the hall swung open. A wave of cold air swept through the room and over Miss Stanford's shoulder Charlie saw a stout figure shuffle inside, wrapped in a long winter overcoat and scarf. He wore an old-fashioned trilby hat, which he lifted it in exaggerated greeting.

'I do 'ope I'm not interruptin' your rehearsal, Miss

Stanford.' Arnold Cartwright flashed his yellow smile.

'Not at all, Mr Cartwright,' said Miss Stanford. 'We were just taking a break.'

'Then I've come at a good moment,' he said. 'By the way, 'ow is your mother and that great big 'ouse of hers?'

'She is doing as well as can be expected,' came the brisk reply.

'Well, if you need it clearin' out when the time comes, you know where I am. Now if you'll excuse me, I was hopin' to 'ave a word with this young man.'

Miss Stanford looked at him with something close to disgust. 'I'm sure Charlie can spare you a few minutes, but backstage. We need to start again in here in a moment.'

Mr Cartwright nodded and beckoned to Charlie, who set down his paintbrush warily and followed the antique dealer to a cramped room behind the stage. Cartwright lowered himself into a chair beside a rack of musty stage costumes. The air was stale and cold.

'Now young man, I was wonderin' if you'd 'ad any further thoughts about our conversation yesterday?' His piggy eyes gleamed.

'How did you know where to find me?'

Cartwright shrugged. 'It's a small place. Not

many secrets round 'ere. But never mind that. About that brass box of yours, the one you brought into the shop.' He leaned towards Charlie, who caught a reek of coffee breath. 'I'm willing to make you a final offer for it: one 'undred pounds.'

Charlie let out a tiny gasp and Cartwright smiled.

'Yes, one 'undred pounds in cash. But I need the box now.'

The distant sound of the children's singing drifted from the front of the hall.

'I haven't got it with me,' Charlie said. 'It's in my room at Darkwater House.'

'Is it now?' Mr Cartwright rubbed his chin slowly. 'And which room is that? I was invited to clear some rooms in that 'ouse years ago. Full of junk. Nothin' worth much.'

'I'm in the attic room at the back.'

'Are you now?' He thought for a moment. 'I remember it. Well, I can just wait here while you run back and get it. Or I can take you back there myself. My car's just outside and I've got the money 'ere.'

He tapped his coat pocket.

'Why do you want it so much, Mr Cartwright?'

Arnold Cartwright removed his glasses and polished the lenses with a dark silk handkerchief.

'This is a strange little part of the world and so we 'ave our own quirky pieces of local 'istory,' he said. 'I think that box may well be one of 'em. Plenty of ships have run aground on the sandbanks or come to grief on the Serpent's Tongue rocks, and so occasionally things turn up that are of...interest... 'Ave you opened it, by the way?'

Charlie shook his head. 'I can't. The lock's all jammed up. What do you think's in it?'

The antique dealer shrugged. 'There's one local tale, the story of a little passenger steamship that was lost on a return voyage from the continent years ago. People still talk about it. In fact there's a famous picture of it in the town museum.' He corrected himself. 'Famous by Dunstrand standards, at least.'

'What happened?'

Cartwright replaced his glasses and waved his hand vaguely as if he were dismissing his own story. Charlie had the sudden sense this air of nonchalance was an act.

'The rumour always was that some rich fella from London was on board and he drowned when the ship ran aground out on the Serpent's Teeth sandbanks in a storm. A few of 'is possessions ended up in the sea, or so they say. It's possible that box might be one of 'em. Nothin' more than a little local gossip and of interest only to those of us who live in these parts.'

'Really? I bet some of the antique dealers back in London would be interested.'

Cartwright shook his head. 'I very much doubt it. As I said, it's a local curiosity, nothin' more. But you always need to be prepared to take a chance in my line of work. I think you'll find my offer is extremely generous.'

Charlie thought for a moment. One hundred pounds... He could get those new football boots his mum wouldn't buy him because she said they were too expensive. And there might still be enough for him and Sanjay to get a pizza.

Cartwright leaned closer and there was a sudden menace in his words. 'This is your last chance, young man. And let me give you some advice. You should know one thing: I always get what I want in the end.'

Charlie felt suddenly very alone. The singing in the hall had stopped. Cartwright pulled his wallet from his inside pocket and slowly set down five twenty-pound notes on the table. The piggy eyes blinked back at him, waiting.

'Stuff your money!'

They both turned to the doorway in surprise to

see Ariel, hands on hips.

'And who are you?' Cartwright said.

'I'm his cousin. And I'm telling you, Charlie doesn't want anything to do with you.' She stared at him defiantly.

'Now my dear, this young man and I 'ave already agreed a price—'

'One – don't patronise me. Two – you've agreed nothing. Three – I don't know what you're up to, but I bet you're taking advantage of him. Charlie doesn't know you, he's not from round here, but everyone else does. So why don't you just leave him alone?'

Cartwright looked at the fierce figure glaring at him as if trying to work out if she was bluffing. He got slowly to his feet, his expression as hard as the winter ground outside.

'Very well, but you are both extremely foolish children to turn down my offer – and even more so to cross me. And you'd better watch your words, young lady. There's such a thing as slander you know. You keep them nasty opinions to yourself if you know what's good for you. You haven't 'eard the last of this. Mark my words.'

He slammed the door and the children could hear his shuffling steps echoing down the hallway.

Charlie's legs felt unsteady.

'Are you all right?' said Ariel.

'Yes, fine. Probably the paint fumes. You just cost me one hundred quid, you know.'

'Lucky escape more like. You don't want to get involved with him. People round here can't stand him.' She frowned. 'Why was he offering you money anyway?'

He began to tell her about his find on the beach, but before they could discuss it any further, Miss Stanford put her head round the door.

'There you both are! I need your help to move some of the scenery so we can work out exactly where the children need to stand for the finale.'

'Sorry. We're coming now,' said Ariel. 'Charlie, you can tell me the rest on the way home.'

———◇———

Heavy grey clouds were rolling in with the evening as they walked back from town and along the lane to Darkwater House. The wind had a bitter edge, rustling the bare branches of the trees that overhung the driveway. A light burned in the outhouse and through the window they could see Uncle Patrick crouched over his work bench, surrounded by newly painted mugs.

Ariel pushed open the front door of the house. It was not locked.

'That's quite a story, Charlie,' she said, as he reached the end of it. 'I'd like to see this box for myself.'

'It's upstairs.'

Her eyes shone. 'Let's open it now!'

'I'm not sure. It's all seized up for one thing, and then... Well, I just don't think we should. That old man I was telling you about, he was pretty certain. He said I should just chuck it straight back in the sea.'

'Do you always do what you're told?'

Charlie considered. He was no saint at school but had certainly learned that keeping your nose clean led to a quieter life. And frankly he was all for that.

But Ariel was already halfway up the stairs, hurrying to the top of the house. Entering Charlie's room, she sat down cross-legged and impatient as he rummaged reluctantly in the wardrobe. The box was still there, wrapped up where he had left it. Gingerly, he passed it over to her. 'I'm still not sure this is a great idea.'

Ariel held it up to the light and read the inscription out loud. '*All the devils are here*. That's from *The Tempest*.'

'What?'

'It's a quotation from Shakespeare. From his play *The Tempest*.'

'How do you know that?'

'It was my mother's favourite. She had this picture-book version she used to read to me. How do you think I ended up with a name like this?'

'I thought it was something to do with that kids' film.'

She rolled her eyes and turned the box over in her hands. 'Look at that engraving on the lid.' She traced it with her finger. 'I bet that's supposed to be the spirit Ariel imprisoned inside a pine tree by the witch Sycorax.'

Charlie looked at her blankly.

'The witch is the mother of the monster Caliban. At the start of the play they – oh never mind. This box sounds empty. Have you even tried to open it?'

'I told you, you can't. The lock is all jammed up.'

Ariel examined the lock under the light. 'I reckon we can smash that open. There's a hammer and chisel in the toolbox under the stairs.'

'I don't think we should.'

Ariel gave him the pitying look she reserved for dealings with her father. 'Why not? Don't you want to see what's in there?'

'But that old man said it was dangerous and I should get rid of it.'

'Oh come on!' Ariel scrambled to her feet. 'There's got to be a reason why Cartwright came to find you and offer you a hundred quid. Let's get it open.'

Before he could object, his cousin was off down the stairs and back a few moments later with a metal toolbox under her arm. Ferdinand the cat padded in though the open door behind her and, with an effort, jumped up onto the window ledge as if settling in to watch. Behind him, the great branches of the tree swayed in the wind. Ariel knelt on the floor beside Charlie, setting a chisel and hammer down on the carpet beside him.

'Do you want to do it?' she asked. 'You found it.'

'What if we break it?'

'If you're frightened, I'll do it.'

Charlie grabbed the tools. He was fed up with that word. 'I'm not frightened.'

Ariel smiled and he felt annoyed at how easily she had managed to goad him into action.

'Come on then,' she said. 'I'll hold it steady for you. Let's get this treasure box of yours open.'

She flipped it over so that the rusted clasp was

facing upwards and took a firm grip on the sides.

Charlie poked the blade of the chisel into the lock and gave it a gentle couple of taps like he was knocking on the headmaster's office door.

'Oh, come on Charlie!' said Ariel, exasperated. 'Do you want to open it or not?'

He hit it again, harder this time, but the blade slipped from the lock, leaving it firmly in place.

'Let me have a go,' said Ariel, swiping the hammer. 'Here, you hold this. And keep your fingers out of the way.'

She drew back her arm and smashed the hammer as if she were driving in a tent peg with a mallet. Charlie winced. Ferdinand retreated to the far corner of the windowsill, taking refuge behind the curtain. At the third blow there was a loud crack and the lock burst open.

Very gently, Ariel eased back the lid.

And then she laughed.

'What is it?'

'Nothing! Your famous box is empty I'm afraid. Perhaps you should have taken the money after all.'

Charlie peered inside, relieved and disappointed.

'Hold on a minute.' He scratched his finger against something wedged tightly in the corner of the box. With some effort, he worked it free. A tiny silver disc attached to a chain nestled in the palm of his hand. He poked it gently with his index finger. It was plain, thin and stained with age.

Ariel snorted. 'Is that it? A little medallion? Not much to write home about.'

Charlie shook the box. 'Nothing else.'

'Well, finders keepers, Charlie. It's yours.'

He twisted the chain round his fingers. 'Maybe it will bring us good luck.'

At that moment they heard Uncle Patrick's voice calling from the hall: 'Ariel! Charlie! Want to come into town to get some chips for dinner?'

Charlie scrambled to his feet. 'I'm starving!'

'OK, we're coming,' Ariel yelled back down the stairs. 'No need to shout.'

Charlie stuffed the medallion into his pocket and placed the box back on the window ledge. Ferdinand jumped out from behind the curtain and they followed him down to the hall.

'Don't forget your coats,' Uncle Patrick said, patting his pockets for the car keys. 'It's gone really cold out there.'

'I'm sure I'll survive,' Ariel replied.

'My coat's upstairs,' said Charlie. 'Can you hold

on a minute?'

'We won't be going anywhere if I can't find my keys. Maybe I left them in the outhouse. I'll go and check. How about we all meet out front in five minutes?'

Back up in his room, Charlie found his coat in the tangle of unmade bedsheets and put it on, along with his beanie hat. He stood in the doorway and turned out the light, but as he did so, something stopped him in his tracks. A faint blue light cast a glow over the walls. It seemed to be coming from the open box on the window ledge. He snapped the main light back on but all he could see was the slightest wisp of pale smoke rising up from the box and into the room. It curled around the ceiling for a moment like mist on water, shifting and twisting through the air before finally vanishing into the depths of the house.

Charlie blinked hard, unsure if he had imagined it, and then went tentatively over to take a closer look. The box was just as they had left it: open and empty. He bit his lip uneasily and was grateful for the reassuring sounds of Uncle Patrick in the hall.

'Right! Found the keys. Come on, you two. Let's go.'

CHAPTER ELEVEN

Later that evening, the Christmas tree shuddered in its bucket and Patrick emerged from behind it with a frown. 'It's still not straight.'

Ariel looked up from the floor, surrounded by a pile of cardboard boxes with tissue paper spread out all around. 'Can we just get on with it please?'

'Hold the base for me, Charlie.'

His uncle shook the trunk once more and, satisfied at last, he stepped back to admire his work. 'Got it.'

A fire was burning in the grate and the soft lamps threw pools of light into the corners of the room. The smell of the freshly cut tree mingled with the dust from the boxes they had carried down from the attic after dinner, which the children were now rummaging through. Charlie sneezed.

'I came across these decorations when I was on the roof during the summer, trying to patch up a leak,' Uncle Patrick said. 'They must have been left by someone who lived here once.' He pulled out a faded paper-chain of tiny angels. 'Some of this stuff hasn't seen the light of day for years. Should be in a museum, this one.'

Next came a string of coloured lights but when Ariel plugged them in, nothing happened. Patrick went to find a screwdriver.

'Ugh! What's that?' Charlie pulled a face as he opened the last cardboard box. Sitting on top of the tissue paper was what looked like a thin strip of brown material, but on closer inspection it had whiskers and a tail.

'That's weird,' Ariel said, crouching down beside him like a zoologist in the field. 'It's a mouse. Or it was.'

The creature was dead, crushed flat as if it had been struck with a hammer, but there was not a spot of blood anywhere on it. Its black eyes stared blankly.

'What happened to it?'

'I don't know. Usually Ferdinand rips them to bits but this one looks like it's had the life sucked out of it.'

Carefully, she wrapped the body in tissue paper and dropped it into the fire. A bright flame flared in the grate.

'Viking burial.'

Charlie wrinkled his nose.

'Let's have some music.' Patrick returned with a glass of wine in one hand and a screwdriver in the other. 'Put the radio on, Charlie.'

There was a big, old-fashioned set on one of the bookshelves beside the fire. The knobs turned with a satisfying click.

'You have to twiddle them to find a station.'

'Doesn't it have pre-sets?'

Uncle Patrick shook his head. 'You kids…'

Charlie twisted the dial and out of the static came the sudden burble of foreign voices, then the sound of a violin and finally the singing of a Christmas choir. The music had a thin quality to it, as if it had travelled many miles through the winter night to reach this remote room; Charlie listened, mesmerised by the sweet sound and the white glow of the dial. Together he and his cousin decorated the tree, with the music playing quietly.

Uncle Patrick worked on the string of lights, looking up from time to time.

'Ariel, don't stand on the steps without Charlie holding them. They're a bit rickety.'

'Relax! I'm only two feet up!'

Charlie swiftly grabbed the step ladder before the conversation got any more heated.

He watched as Ariel added some baubles to the higher branches. Uncle Patrick let out a little cheer when he tested the lights and passed them over to Ariel to twist round the tree.

All of a sudden, Charlie felt the sharp and unexpected bite of homesickness. It was as if he had been ambushed by the music and the scent of the pine needles. In that moment, he wished again that he was back in London listening to the scratch of his mother's fountain pen as she did her Christmas cards at the kitchen table while his father fretted over the pastry for his mince pies. Charlie dug his nails into his palms and squeezed his fists tight. The vision dissolved.

'Now there are a few special ones in here.' Patrick took down a single shoebox from the bookshelf. 'Just a couple of things that came back from India with us.'

'The Elephant Bauble!' Ariel beamed as she pulled it free. The decoration was dark red with a delicate parade of painted golden elephants marching in line around it with their trunks and tails entwined.

'Your mum gave you that for your first Christmas.'

She smiled and gently held it up to the light by

the thin piece of thread at the top. It turned slowly in her hand. 'I'll put it high up.'

Ariel started to climb the steps, which wobbled slightly. Uncle Patrick went over to steady them but as he did so, he accidentally nudged her leg just as she was reaching out to hang the bauble on the tree. Charlie watched it slip from her hand and hit the hearth with a crack, shattering against the stone.

'Look what you've made me do!' Ariel shouted.

'I was just trying to make sure that...'

'You are always interfering! You never trust me to do anything on my own!' She glared at her father, her cheeks red with rage. 'Why can't you just leave me alone?'

Uncle Patrick looked incredulous. 'Leave you alone? You're always doing your own thing.'

'How can you say that? You're always in my face.'

'Ariel, I'm your father. I'm supposed to look out for you. It's what I do.'

'Shame you didn't do that for Mum.'

The words slashed through the air like a butcher's knife across a carcass. Ariel glared at her father, who slowly began to rub his face with his hands, as if fighting hard to ignore the provocation and control himself. But he could not.

Charlie slipped into the hall leaving the sounds of their furious argument behind. He hurried outside and kept going, watching the raw wind chase dead leaves around the yard. It was too dark to head down the track to the sea, even if he had the courage to try, so he found himself wandering towards the outbuildings in need of company. Bobby was in his stall, peering out into the field that stretched away towards the woods and the track that led back to the farm. He shook his mane at Charlie's approach and Charlie patted his neck, firmly and with confidence.

'Hello, boy.' He felt embarrassed, talking to an animal. But there was no one around to hear, so he continued. 'They're at it again! I wish they could get along better. It's no good for anyone, this.'

The horse pushed its damp nose into Charlie's hand, nudging at his palm.

'You want something to eat? I don't think I've got anything.' He shoved his hand into his pocket and came out with an ancient mint, covered in fluff. The horse's rough tongue licked it eagerly from his hand. 'You like that? I'll see if I've got anything else.'

In the weak light, he turned out the rest of his pockets but found only an old paper tissue and the little medallion from inside the brass box. 'Sorry, you can't eat that. Although…' He looked at the tiny trinkets that Ariel had sewn into the horse's winter jacket and an idea came to him. He reached over and tied the medallion to a loop in the fabric, where it clinked alongside some of the other decorations. 'There you go. A Christmas present from me to you.'

The horse shook its head and turned the straw idly with its hooves. Charlie patted him once more and, in that moment, he understood why his cousin loved the animals around her: she trusted them completely and they her. There were no arguments or accidents: it was a relationship of total simplicity.

Over in the house, a light came on in the kitchen. At the window, Uncle Patrick stood at the sink, staring blankly into the night.

'I should probably go in,' Charlie whispered. 'Time for bed.'

He walked back to the house, hearing the horse swish its tail and shuffle its hooves in the darkness behind him.

Inside, his uncle was apologetic.

'I'm sorry about all that,' he sighed. 'I think everyone's very tired. It's a stressful time of year. And I was only trying to help. I'm only ever trying to help.'

'It's OK,' Charlie said.

'Ariel's gone up to bed. I'll head up too, in a minute. Got to be up early for the Christmas Fair over King's Lynn way tomorrow. It's a bit of a trek and it's not fair to drag you both all the way out there. Not that I think Ariel would even want to come after this evening.' He puffed out his cheeks. 'And the weather forecast isn't great. Snow on the way, they think.'

Charlie could see his uncle was uneasy at the prospect of the trip. Not so much the weather, he guessed, but at the very idea of going away and leaving his daughter, just as he had done in India once before.

'Still, it's one of the biggest markets around,' Patrick continued, as much to himself as to Charlie. 'A good day there will set me up for a months. And there's Christmas to pay for. Got to do it.'

'Will we see you in the morning?'

'Probably not. I'll be gone pretty much all day and most of the evening. Will you two be all right together? I did think you seemed to be getting along a little better now.'

'Yeah. We're fine,' said Charlie.

Uncle Patrick rubbed his beard with both hands. 'My daughter can be so infuriating at times. I'm sorry.'

'You should stop worrying so much. She's all right. I promise you.'

'I hope so, Charlie. I really do...' Uncle Patrick stared into the embers of the stove for a moment, then shook his head briskly. 'I've a couple of things I still need to sort out in the studio for tomorrow. I'll shut everything up down here when I'm done. Sleep well.' He went out through the back door and disappeared into the dark.

The light from the newly decorated Christmas tree spilled out into the hallway as Charlie reached the foot of the stairs. He could not resist a final look at their handiwork before bed, and so he pushed open the sitting room door. The tree stood beside the fireplace in a halo of light, the heavy aroma of its fresh needles mixing with the smoking log in the grate. Charlie pushed his nose up close to the branches to breathe in the smell of Christmas.

As he did so, something caught his eye, reflected in the polished surface of one of the baubles. He froze. Standing behind him, over his shoulder, was a man with a blistered face and blank eye sockets, mouth contorted into a great gaping snarl. Charlie screamed and whirled round, stumbling as he did so, but when he scrambled back to his feet and looked again, the room was empty and the only sound was the dying fire, hissing in the grate.

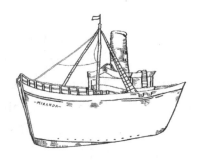

CHAPTER TWELVE

Somewhere, a clock struck three. The sound filtered into Charlie's ragged sleep and he was awake once more, the terrible reflection still hovering on the edges of his mind. He sat up with effort, unwinding himself from the knot of the sheets, and turned on the light.

The box sat on the windowsill, its lid raised. There was something unsettling about it, as if it were watching him. He took a deep breath to calm himself. Ariel had been so dismissive when they had opened it, so certain that there was nothing untoward in what he had found. And if she felt like that, why didn't he? Maybe it was that weird light he thought he had seen coming from it, and of course she had not been there when he had first found it, pulling it out from the sand in which it had lain buried for all those years.

He slid out of bed and went over to the box, peering closely at the carvings in the brass. His head began to swim with the strange images and suddenly, for a brief moment, he felt an overwhelming sense of rage and anger sweep over him, as if he had walked past a fire and felt a short blast of its heat; but then the sensation subsided as quickly as it had come. He snapped the lid of the box down hard and retreated to bed. Was this what it was like to lose your mind? Was this how it began?

And then the noise started. Almost imperceptible at first, drifting in from along the corridor, and so faint that he wondered if he might be dreaming again, but as he lay there he knew the sounds were as real as the walls around him. This was different from anything he had heard before and the next thing he knew he was hurrying down the passageway, the light from his phone illuminating the bare carpet and his scurrying feet. He rapped on Ariel's bedroom door.

'Wake up!' Charlie hissed. 'You have to come and listen to this!'

There was no answer. After a moment, he turned the handle gently and stepped inside. On the far side of the room, Ariel rolled over in her bed, murmuring something in that half-state between waking and sleeping. He took a step towards her, a floorboard creaked and she suddenly sat bolt upright.

'Ariel? Are you OK?' Charlie hissed.

Her eyes were staring straight ahead into the darkness, unseeing: she was still asleep but then she began to speak, her voice low.

'Shh! I'm listening for the sea! Can you hear it? Not the one out there; the real sea. The warm sea with the bright sunlight and the coloured fish. There they are! Look!'

She pointed into the blackness and Charlie dared not break her trance.

'And look at the sand! Yes, I shall wait here for my mother.' She began to sing softly. *'Come unto these yellow sands and then take hands...* She will be here soon. I know she will. I shall sit down and wait for her.'

Her voice slowed gradually until she finally lowered herself back onto her pillow and lay still. Charlie watched her, transfixed. Then, without warning, she sat bolt upright and screamed.

He ran to comfort her, but she pushed him away, shaking.

'It's me, Charlie!' he said. 'You're OK. It was a dream. You were just dreaming.'

In the dim light from the window, he could see her

eyes shining, taking in the solid surroundings of the room as it materialised around her. When she spoke, her voice had recovered some of its old strength. She blinked hard.

'What's the matter?' she asked. 'Why are you here?'

Charlie said simply: 'You have to come and listen to this.'

She pulled on an old sweatshirt from beside her bed and followed him down the passageway in the dark. They stopped outside the empty bedroom close to Charlie's attic.

'I heard them again. The ghost children.'

'Is that what you got me up for? They can't hurt you. I told you, they're just playing.'

'Not this time.'

Charlie strained his ears but heard nothing except the clicking of a water pipe somewhere in the dark. Then it began again. Not laughter this time, but the gentle sobbing of a child.

'You told me they were always happy,' Charlie said, 'but listen. Now they're not.'

Ariel looked puzzled.

The sobbing grew louder as if the child were growing more and more distressed. Then came another voice, a little boy's this time, whispering urgently in the dark.

'*He is here! He is here! We must not let him find us! He is here in our home!*'

'What are they talking about?' Charlie's eyes were wide and white.

Ariel pressed her ear to the door. 'I don't know. I've never heard them speak like this before. They are always laughing or playing. Something must have happened.'

'*He is here! We must not let him find us! He is here in our home!*'

'Who is here?'

Ariel shook her head, then seized the door handle. She burst in, turning on the light, but the room was empty and the voices were silent.

'What were you expecting to find?'

'I don't know.'

'*He is here,*' Charlie repeated slowly. 'Who is here?'

'I've no idea. Are you all right? You look terrible.'

'I haven't slept much.' He tried to keep his voice steady as he told her about the reflection in the bauble as he had come up to bed.

'I've got some sweets in my room if you want one before you go back to sleep. Might make you feel better.'

Charlie sat on the end of her bed while Ariel

hunted through the bottom of her wardrobe. Her bedroom had a high ceiling with a wide window running across its length. Through the crack in the curtains, he could see she had filled the sill with red velvet cushions to make a reading seat.

She tossed him a packet of sweets and sat cross-legged on the big armchair in the centre of the room with a packet of her own. 'I like the green ones best.'

'Really? I can't stand those. Red are way better.'

They crunched in silence for a moment and Charlie looked round, able to take in the surroundings properly at last. There was a sewing machine in one corner, surrounded by scraps of fabric and thread and pictures torn from fashion magazines. A half-finished dress was draped across the back of a chair beside a tiny toy rabbit, grimy and missing an ear. One wall was covered in charcoal sketches of horses and birds, punctuated with recurring portraits of Ariel's mother, and there was a photograph of her in a silver frame beside the bed.

He felt her watching him.

'She was very beautiful,' he said finally.

Ariel's dark eyes were wet with tears.

'I'm sorry,' he whispered. 'I didn't mean to upset you.'

She blinked hard and two teardrops slid in unison

down her cheeks and met at her chin.

'Have you ever wanted something so much it hurts? Something that no matter what you do, you can't have?'

He considered for a second. 'I don't think so. Unless you count…you know, football or something.'

She laughed and wiped her face with her sleeve.

'You're lucky, Charlie. If that's how it is for you, you're really lucky. These sketches,' she waved at the pictures of her mother, 'they come to me all the time. I have the pictures in my head.'

'You must miss her,' Charlie balled his toes tightly under the blanket, embarrassed by his failure to find the right words.

'Every single day. I dream about her too.'

'I know.'

She looked at him quizzically but continued.

'She was very beautiful and kind. She used to read to me in French – she was born in Paris – and it's weird. I sometimes dream about her reading to me and I can hear all the words in my head and I can understand them all. And sometimes in French lessons at school I'm not very good, and then other times it all just spills out of me like I'm a native, and I don't know how all the words and phrases got

137

in there.'

He unwrapped another sweet from the bag. 'What do you miss most? What would you do if she was here right now?'

Ariel pulled her knees up to her chest and wrapped her arms around them. 'I would just give her the longest, tightest most amazing hug you could ever imagine. It would be...' her voice quivered, 'the best there's ever been.'

They sat silently for a moment listening to the wind in the trees outside the window. And later, when Charlie went back to bed, he left her still sitting there, quietly staring at a slice of moonlight falling across the bedroom floor.

CHAPTER THIRTEEN

The kitchen window was etched with frost as Charlie sat eating his breakfast. He was wearing his coat and, in the absence of wi-fi, was leafing through a book about fishing that he had found on a shelf in the study. The illustrations were surprisingly good and he found himself idly wondering about hiring a rod one day next summer. His dad might enjoy that too.

His daydream was a pleasant distraction from the disturbances of the night. With the bright winter light at the window and thick slices of toast and honey on his plate, the world suddenly seemed reassuringly normal. A firm grip on his emotions was what he needed. Just a few more days. Then it would be Christmas Eve and time to go home with his dad. Leave all this behind. He returned to his book, but was immediately disturbed by Ariel clattering in through the back door and throwing her riding hat down on the table.

'What's up?' he asked.

There was a tremor in her voice. 'Ferdinand's dead.'

Charlie hurried out after her into the courtyard, closing the back door behind him.

'I was out early to feed Bobby and ride him back up to the farm,' she explained, 'and I found Ferdinand when I was walking back.' She knelt down beside an old sack which was resting next to the door of Uncle Patrick's studio. Gently, she unwrapped its folds.

'He was lying in the lane.'

The old cat was on his side, eyes wide open and tongue protruding slightly from his mouth. The effect was unnerving: it looked as if he were screaming. His fur was unmarked, but his entire body and tail were stretched out thin and dehydrated, sucked dry of all blood and life.

'What happened to him? Was he hit by a car?'

'I don't think so. There isn't a scratch on him.'

A nameless unease stirred in Charlie's stomach. Something was very wrong: the grumpy old guardian of Darkwater House did not deserve to have his days cut short like this.

'It's just like that mouse,' he said.

'What do you mean?'

'The mouse we found among the Christmas decorations last night. Remember? That looked the same.'

'But what would do something like that?'

'Something that was hungry?'

They decided to bury Ferdinand under the apple tree at the front of the house. Ariel said it had been one of his favourite places to nap during the heat of summer. He had sat there watching them move in, yawning at his latest set of tenants. He would like it there. They re-wrapped the sack and together they carried the cat's body in a solemn little cortege over the front lawn to the tree by the gate.

Charlie pushed a spade into the cold ground, cutting though the frosty grass and into the black earth beneath. It was hard work and he dug in silence for a while. Once he looked up and caught Ariel dabbing her eyes with her sleeve. After last night, he felt certain his cousin was too proud to let him see her cry again, so he said nothing, his spade chinking against hidden stones.

After a while, he paused his digging to catch his breath. It was then that he saw a flash of light from the field opposite the house. It was brief, like the sun reflecting off a closing window, and then something moved in the hedgerow, scuttling quickly back under the cover of the trees.

'Someone's watching us,' said Charlie.

Ariel followed his gaze. 'I can't see anything. You sure you're feeling OK?'

'I'm fine,' Charlie said, suddenly irritated at being cast in the role of the younger cousin who could not cope. 'Someone was standing on the edge of the field. I'm sure of it.' He scanned the hedges again, but could see nothing. 'Does anyone know we're on our own here today?'

Ariel shrugged. 'Everyone I expect. They know Dad does all those Christmas fairs and the one he's at today is the biggest of the lot.'

Charlie stared at the field once more. A pair of wood pigeons flapped up from the top of the lane that led to the house. Warily, he returned to his task.

Eventually the grave was dug, shining damp and smelling like a cellar. A pink worm writhed at the bottom. Together they lifted the sack and laid Ferdinand gently inside.

'Do you want to say something?' Charlie asked, wondering if the moment demanded it.

'No. It's all done now. But I will find old Ferdinand some flowers.'

She began a sad circuit of the front garden, pulling a winter posy from the hedge and borders while Charlie filled the grave. As he finished, Ariel returned with a bouquet of old man's beard and trailing ivy, wrapped around some sprigs of holly. Carefully she placed them on the fresh earth, and they stepped back a respectful pace. The berries were the only brightness amid the palette of winter grey and brown and Charlie's thoughts clouded as he looked down at them: the prospect of another day at Darkwater suddenly filled him with a gnawing anxiety. This place of big skies, strange voices and dead animals was getting inside his head; his confidence from breakfast time was ebbing away.

'We should call someone,' he said.

Ariel looked puzzled. 'Who?'

'Your dad…or someone. A grown-up. Let someone know.'

Ariel snorted. 'We'll tell him when he gets back. Ferdinand isn't going anywhere.' She stood silent, looking down at the grave. Charlie picked up the spade to leave her in peace and wandered back towards the house. But as he turned into the courtyard, he stopped, alert and on edge. The back door of the house was wide open.

'I know I shut that behind me,' he said under his breath. 'I remember doing it.'

He stood staring for a moment but could see no sign of movement inside.

'Ariel!' he hissed. 'Ariel!'

Quietly as he could, he laid down the spade and hurried back to the front garden.

'Someone's been in the house while we've been out here. I think they might still be inside. They got in through the back.'

'Show me!'

They ran across the garden and stopped at the corner of the house, peering round into the courtyard of outbuildings. The back door of the house hung open on its hinges. Nothing moved.

'Come on,' Ariel tugged his sleeve. 'Let's see who's in there.'

She stepped forward quietly and before Charlie had time to object, had made her way to the back wall of the house where she crouched down beside the kitchen window. Charlie hurried after her, afraid the hammering of his heart would give them away to whoever might be lurking inside. She gestured to him to keep silent and carefully straightened up to press her forehead to the glass.

'Can't see anyone in the kitchen. Let's go inside.'

There was a muffled bang from the other side of the house. They looked at each other.

'What was that?'

'The front door! Come on Charlie!'

They raced round the house just in time to catch a glimpse of a man in a hat disappearing around the top of the driveway and scuttling away down the lane, clutching a leather bag in his hand.

'He's heading for the main road,' Charlie shouted.

They hurtled after him but ahead of them, hidden from sight around the bend of the lane, they heard the roar of a car engine starting up.

'Come on!'

They ran as fast as they could but already the sound of the accelerating car was fading away into the distance. Whoever it was had planned his escape with great care.

Ariel stamped the ground in frustration and they returned home despondent and certain of what they would discover once they were inside. Sure enough, as they climbed the stairs to Charlie's attic room, the door was open and the windowsill was bare.

The box had gone.

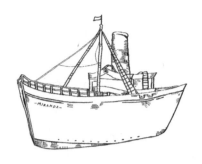

CHAPTER FOURTEEN

When Ariel spoke, her voice was measured and deliberate, the undertone of her anger unmistakable.

'We'll get it back. It doesn't belong to him. He can't just walk into our house and take things.'

'Who can't?'

'It was Cartwright. It must have been him. Did you see the hat? He was wearing one just like it the other day. And he's wanted that box from the moment he saw it. When you wouldn't sell it to him yesterday he decided to take it anyway.'

'But how did he know where it was? There was no way he could—' Charlie stopped himself, recalling the unpleasant conversation with the antique dealer at the back of the church hall. 'I think I might have let it slip by accident.'

Ariel was not listening.

'Nobody can treat me like this and get away with it.'

'Shouldn't we go to the police?'

'And say what? That we think Cartwright's a thief? We don't have any evidence and he'd just deny it. But we know what he's done. We'll have to sort this out ourselves, Charlie.'

A horn sounded suddenly in the lane. David Cooper's tractor stood ticking over by the gates, with Clara and Pebble beside the farmer in the cab.

'Morning!' David waved a greeting as they came outside. 'My mother's got something for you.'

The old lady turned her milky eyes towards the children at the sound of their approach, her hands gently rubbing the fur on the top of her dog's head.

'How are you? I understand Patrick is away today.'

'We're OK, Clara.'

'I am very glad to hear it.' The old lady dipped her hand into a wicker basket on her lap and passed them down two warm cookies wrapped in a paper napkin. 'Freshly baked by my grandchildren this morning. I must not let you starve without your father around.'

They devoured the cookies on the spot, David watching in wry amusement.

'Are you going into Dunstrand?' Ariel asked, wiping her mouth.

David nodded.

'Can we have a lift?'

David jerked his thumb towards the trailer behind the cab. 'Hold on tight to the sides and keep your hands in.'

After Ariel had quickly run back to close the doors of the house, they scrambled up and soon they were bouncing along the road. The height of the trailer gave Charlie a clear view of the beach and the sea.

'What's the rush to get into town?' asked Charlie.

'It's where that car was heading. The road is only surfaced properly in the direction of Dunstrand. The other way it's just a bumpy old track over the headland. So, given the speed it drove off at, it must have been going into town. To Cartwright's place, I'm sure.'

'And what are we going to do then?'

'I'll think of something.'

David shouted from the cab. 'I'm going to drop you two in the market square by the Christmas tree. That all right?'

Charlie gave a thumbs-up.

'Good! Mother has some shopping to do and I need to pick up some more chicken wire to fix the fence. We had fox trouble last night.'

'What happened?' Ariel yelled over the noise of the engine.

'Something got into the hen house and we lost three birds. No sign of two of them this morning and there wasn't much left of the third. It was like it had all the life sucked out of it. Never seen anything quite like it.'

The cousins looked at one another, but before they could say any more the tractor had turned into the square. The flint-fronted buildings of the town seemed to be huddling together for warmth that morning, sheltering from the keen wind blowing in from the sea. Overhead, the Christmas lights swayed on their wires, while shoppers hurried beneath, wrapped up with their heads down.

'Thanks for the lift,' Ariel said, dropping onto the cobbles.

The tractor pulled away and Charlie waved in thanks. 'Weird coincidence about their hens,' he said, watching it disappear.

'It's not a coincidence. First that mouse, then Ferdinand, now their birds. And the ghost children at Darkwater being so upset...'

Charlie looked at her. 'And you know when all this started? Right after we opened the box.' He hesitated, suddenly afraid. That faint glow he had seen coming from it when he returned to his attic room alone; the wisp of something escaping out into the house... Maybe it was good the box had gone. Perhaps it was better to have nothing more to do with it. But he could see the fierce set of his cousin's eyes: in her mind someone had violated her home, stealing something precious, and she would never let that injustice go unpunished.

'Look,' said Charlie, 'I think maybe I did see something a little weird after we'd opened the box.'

Ariel listened as he explained it to her, then she said simply: 'That's why we need to get it back. There's more to that box than we thought – and nobody gets away with stealing stuff from me.'

'Should we tell—'

'Please don't say a grown-up, Charlie! That's your answer to everything. What use are they? When have they ever helped me? We'll sort this ourselves, just like I said.'

She marched off across the square and Charlie watched her go. Her single-mindedness scared him sometimes, but he could not face any of this alone. Or abandon her now.

'Hey, Ariel. Wait for me!'

He ran to catch up, past the church hall and down the narrow street that led to the harbour, where the boats lay like listless seals on the muddy shore, waiting for the turn of the tide. Together the cousins ducked down beside the sea wall where they had a view of the little parade of shops which included Cartwright's Antiques. Behind them, two gulls fought noisily over a dead fish, pecking holes in its side.

'So what's the plan?' Charlie asked.

Inside the shop they could see a few customers browsing the shelves, while at the till, Miss Timms wrapped a parcel in tissue paper.

Ariel squeezed Charlie's arm and hurriedly pulled him closer against the wall without saying a word. Away to their right a line of cars was queuing to get into the car park on the quay, where there seemed to be a problem with the automatic barrier. One driver was impatiently sounding his horn, while another leaned out of his window berating a man in a yellow jacket about the delay. Pushing through the traffic, with obvious impatience, was Arnold Cartwright. Under his hat his face was red, as though he were still trying to catch his breath from some earlier exertion, and there was a sheen of sweat on his brow. Round his neck was a pair of binoculars and in his hand a small leather bag. He hurried along the pavement opposite and into his shop, but if he had hoped to scurry away into the privacy of his office, his plan was thwarted. A customer stepped immediately in front of him and pointed at a something in the window. Reluctantly, Cartwright put the bag down on the counter and shuffled over to serve him.

'I bet he's got the box in that bag,' said Charlie.

Ariel smiled. 'Then let's go in and take it back.'

She grabbed her cousin's hand and pulled him over the road, timing their arrival just as one of the customers left. They slipped through the open door and concealed themselves behind the leaves of an aspidistra plant tucked away at the back of the shop. Charlie's heart was beating so loudly that for the second time that day he feared the sound of it might reveal their hiding place. Cartwright was just a few yards from them, in conversation with the customer by the window. The irritation in his voice was clear: yes, it was part of a set; no, he could not offer a discount.

Suddenly they heard another voice behind them: 'I'll see if we have one in the storeroom.' It was Miss Timms, and Charlie felt Ariel's body tense beside him.

'Get down,' his cousin whispered. 'She's coming this way.'

The children crouched further behind the plant pot as Miss Timms' shoes clicked past. Charlie stared at a crack in the floor and wished he could slip down inside it. How would they explain what they were doing here if they were discovered? There was no way Cartwright would believe they were just browsing. He would sense trouble, probably call the police and accuse them of shoplifting.

'Miss Timms!' Cartwright's voice was heavy with frustration. 'Where's the key for the window cabinet? It's not on the 'ook.'

The footsteps paused. 'I have it here, Mr Cartwright.'

'Well what are you doing with it there? I've got a customer waitin'!'

Her footsteps turned and moved away. Ariel took that as her cue to rise silently to her feet, her face glowing with nervous energy. 'Now they're both distracted, here's the plan,' she whispered in Charlie's ear. She pointed at the suit of armour a few feet away in its alcove. 'Shove that over when I tell you. And when they both come over to see what's happened, I'll grab the bag from the counter and make a run for it.'

'What about me?'

'You're going to have to run too.' Her eyes were

wild. 'Race you back to the house.'

Charlie's legs felt weak.

Cartwright had finished serving the customer by the window and was now attempting to usher her out of the door. 'Miss Timms, I think it's time we shut up shop for lunch,' he said.

'But it's not one o'clock yet, Mr Cartwright.'

'Think of it as an early Christmas present.'

Miss Timms looked surprised, but before she could speak again, Cartwright propelled her towards the door as well. 'Come on, before I change my mind. We're closin' for lunch, ladies and gents!' he shouted, shepherding the last customer to the exit. 'Get your coat, Miss Timms. I'll lock up.'

From their hiding place, Charlie saw a flash of concern cross his cousin's face: their escape route was being shut off before their eyes.

'That's it, Miss Timms. See you at two.'

His assistant had barely set foot on the pavement before Cartwright had turned the key in the lock and slipped it into his pocket. Then he flipped the sign on the door round to 'Closed'. The cousins were trapped.

Cartwright, believing himself to be alone at last, licked his lips as he took the leather bag from beside the till.

'What do we do now?' Charlie whispered.

'We've got to hide. He'll see us if we stay here.'

But it was too late: Cartwright was heading straight for them. There was nothing to do but retreat through the gloom until they found themselves up against the back wall of the shop. This time, there was no way out.

Just then there was a loud banging at the front door. Cartwright paused and swore under his breath.

'We're closed!' he shouted.

Ariel grabbed Charlie's hand. She had spotted that the door to Cartwright's private office was ajar. 'Quick, in here.'

A rattling came again from the street as someone tried the handle once again.

'Can't you read the sign?' Cartwright bellowed. 'We're closed until two!'

Whoever was outside must have got the message because then a heavy silence fell over the shop, broken only by the sound of Arnold Cartwright shuffling down the aisle and stepping inside his office.

CHAPTER FIFTEEN

''Ello my beauties,' said Cartwright, 'What do you think of this, then?'

He raised the leather bag to the tank in the corner where six fat, grey fish turned slowly in the water, yellow eyes unblinking. The steady hum of the air filter filled the room and the lights inside the tank bathed everything in a marine glow.

Gently, Cartwright placed the bag on his desk, unzipped it and sank his hands inside. 'Now then, let's get a proper look at you.'

He lifted out the box with both hands, savouring its shape and weight. He ran his fingers over the inscription and snorted under his breath: 'Devils, eh? Superstitious nonsense.'

One of the fish rose slowly to the surface, its fat lips sucking.

''Ungry are you?' Now the box was in his grasp

Cartwright seemed content to draw out the moment of his triumph a little longer. From a shelf above him he took down a red tube and sprinkled a pinch of powder onto the surface of the water. Immediately the fish surged upwards, turning and churning in a knot of scales and eyes.

Cartwright watched them for a while and then sat down at his desk. He switched on the table lamp and placed the brass box in the light. From the drawer at his side, he pulled out a pair of jeweller's glasses and strapped them to his face, his eyes bulging grotesquely as he examined his prize. So absorbed was he in his task, he did not notice the cupboard door beside him was partly open and from inside, Charlie and Ariel peered out through the crack, hardly daring to breathe.

'Now then,' Cartwright muttered to himself. 'Let's see what devils you've really got for me.' He struggled for a few seconds with the lid of the box and when he finally forced it open he shoved his goggles up to his forehead and swore. 'That damned kid lied to me! He's already opened this and swiped what was inside!'

He turned angrily to his pets. 'What was in it, eh? What did he take from it?' The fish continued their slow circuits, oblivious. Cartwright leaned back in his chair, rubbing the bridge of his nose with finger and thumb.

'Oh Arnold, you old fool, letting it slip through your fingers... This could 'ave made your fortune!' He slammed his fist down on the desk, hard.

It was then that a faint breeze began to stir in the room, as if someone had opened a window somewhere at the front of the shop. A pile of papers on the desk began to rustle and a single sheet blew gently to the floor. Cartwright sat up. A door banged somewhere.

''Ello?' he said. 'Who's there?'

More papers fluttered to the floor. Cartwright got slowly to his feet, the box in his hands.

From their hiding place, the cousins had a clear view of his face as he turned towards the office door. It swung open. Whatever was standing on the threshold caused Cartwright's expression to morph from curiosity to terror. The colour drained from his face and his voice, when it came, was hoarse and weak.

'Who are you? What do you want?'

He stood frozen, staring straight ahead, transfixed.

Then, in an instant, the remaining papers on the

desk swirled up into the air as if caught in a gale, and the books on the shelves began to fly across the room. Cartwright screamed and pulled the box tight to his chest. 'No! This is mine! You can't 'ave it!'

But it was too late.

Pulled by some invisible force, Cartwright was flung across the room, cracking his head violently on the corner of the desk as he fell to the floor. For a fleeting moment, reflected in the mirror on the far wall, Charlie caught sight of a man's face: hollow-eyed and with flesh so blistered and raw that he could glimpse the skull beneath it. Then came a tremendous crash as the glass suddenly shattered and the mirror smashed upon the floor.

After that, all was confusion.

Charlie screamed, then somehow he and Ariel were tumbling out from the cupboard and running through a squall of swirling paper with broken glass crackling under their feet; then into the storeroom where a slit of light shone beneath a half-open garage door on the far wall. Behind them the sound of footsteps grew louder and suddenly a howling wind raged about their ears. They ran towards the door and dived onto the cold concrete floor, squeezing themselves through the gap beneath the door.

Charlie was aware of a ripping sound and the taste of dust in his mouth as he rolled over and out onto the street. And then they were both running as fast as they could without ever daring to look back; their only thought to get as far away from the shop as they possibly could.

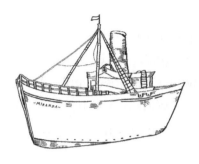

CHAPTER SIXTEEN

Neither of them knew how they ended up on the steps of the town museum, nor how long they stood there, heaving winter air into their lungs. Charlie's hands were shaking, and he pressed them hard against the stone until the adrenaline gradually began to subside. He noticed his coat was torn down the sleeve.

'What happened?' Ariel said to him, at last.

'I don't know. Something was there. Someone. There was a man – but not like a man...' He hesitated. 'Like a ghost. And I've seen him before, reflected in a bauble on the Christmas tree.'

'It wanted the box.'

'Should we go back and help Mr Cartwright? He looked like he was hurt.'

'And have to explain to the police what we were doing in there? No way.'

Charlie looked uncomfortably at his feet. 'I know, but what if he's really badly injured?'

'He got what he deserved,' Ariel said, simply. 'You know what your problem is, Charlie? You're too nice. He didn't care about us, so why should we care about him?'

But Charlie was no longer listening. Instead, he was on his feet, staring intently through the window of the building in front of him. A blue sign in grand letters announced that the Dunstrand Museum & Reading Room was open. He pushed through the front door and headed straight for the far wall where a large oil painting hung in an elaborate gilt frame between the shelves.

'Look!' His voice was an agitated whisper. 'It's the painting of that shipwreck that Cartwright was talking about.'

The canvas showed an old steamship pinned on the Serpent's Teeth sandbanks by mountainous dark waves. There were tiny figures in the water while the little lifeboat of Dunstrand battled the storm to attempt a rescue. In the far corner of the painting, the artist had created a smudge of land with the shape of the lighthouse tower just visible through the spray and cloud. In the foreground, a group of passengers huddled on the deck of the doomed ship while at the prow stood the figure of a solitary man. Painted in bold, black brushstrokes, he was captured in the act of heaving a large bag towards the writhing waves.

'It's him,' Charlie pointed at the figure. 'He's at the heart of all this. He threw the box into the sea all those years ago. He knew what was really in it.'

'You are quite right, young man,' said a voice behind them, making them jump.

They turned to see an old man, his eyes bright and blazing, his face framed with a thick curling white beard. Charlie recognised the figure who had stopped him in the antique shop on that first morning in Dunstrand and who had urged him to throw the box straight back into the sea.

'Who are you? What do you want?' Charlie asked.

'The most pressing question is not who I am, nor what I want,' the old man said steadily, 'but what have *you* done?' He stared at Charlie with those sharp blue eyes. 'Have you got rid of it as I told you to do?'

'Yes, we did,' interrupted Ariel. 'We got rid of it just like you told him.'

The old man turned to her, narrowing his eyes as if trying to establish the truth of her words. Charlie watched her too; she was covering for him and he suddenly felt an overwhelming sense of gratitude for her attempt at protection.

'I do hope so, young lady. I hope for everyone's sake you have done so.'

'Why are you so interested in that box?' Charlie said. 'You seem to be as obsessed with it as Cartwright at the antique shop. There's something nobody is telling us and I'm getting sick of being kept in the dark. That box is special and not one of you is letting on why, because you all want it for yourselves. I reckon it's worth a lot of money.' He could feel the colour rushing to his cheeks. Suddenly he had had enough of them all: this place, these people, everything.

The old man blinked and for the first time Charlie saw a flicker of kindness in his eyes. He ran a hand through his beard as if he were contemplating how much he could trust them. When he spoke, his voice was kinder than before.

'If only it were a simple matter of money, young man.'

'What then?' Charlie demanded. 'Tell us!'

From one of the reading desks by the window someone tutted loudly and hissed for silence.

'Perhaps we had better sit down.' The old man

lowered his voice and gestured to a table scattered with medical journals and a book of local history. He pushed them to one side and Charlie caught sight of the title: *A Study of Witchcraft in East Anglia*.

The old man leaned forward in his chair and began to speak.

'For many years, the rumour around the town was of a wealthy merchant who died in that shipwreck trying to save his expensive cargo.' He nodded towards the picture. 'Some called it the "Serpent's Hoard" and there was fanciful talk of lost diamonds, pearls and gold. When the big ghost tides churned up the beaches in winter, half the town would be down combing the shore to see what they could find. But nothing was ever discovered and over the years people gradually gave up looking. The whole thing passed into local folklore – nothing more than a bit of colour for the guidebooks and history exhibitions. And those beachcombers were wasting their time all along – because there never was any treasure, you see.'

The wail of a siren drifted in from the street as a police car accelerated past the window, heading down the street towards the harbour.

'The truth was far more dangerous. The man

in that painting wasn't a merchant. He was a hero. And he died making sure that box never made it to the shore.'

'Why?' Charlie turned to the picture and the figure on the boat, frozen in time.

'Because he knew it contained something far too dangerous to be carried to land by a well-meaning rescuer. If it had been salvaged, untold horrors could have been unleashed here.' The old man lowered his voice further, so that the children were forced to lean in close to hear. 'He saved this town because that box was, in reality, a prison house. A sealed cell for an evil spirit – a poltergeist, as some prefer to call them. Something that should never be allowed to roam free in this world again. If it ever escaped from that box it would grow strong once more, feeding on the energy of the living things around it until it grew powerful enough to vent its anger upon Dunstrand and everyone in it.'

A few flakes of snow began to drift past the window from the darkening sky.

The old man leaned towards them and pointed a finger in Charlie's face. 'So, when you tell me you've thrown that box into the sea, you had damn well better be telling me the truth.'

CHAPTER SEVENTEEN

It was the flickering blue lights reflecting off the shop windows at the end of the lane that alerted them to the trouble. A crowd had gathered on the cobbles. As Charlie and Ariel peered between the press of bodies, they could see a police car and an ambulance parked outside Cartwright's shop. A flimsy barrier of blue plastic tape flapped in the wind and behind it a policewoman with a sombre face pushed back the more brazen onlookers.

'Please, ladies and gentlemen, move along now. We need to keep this area clear. Thank you.'

Through the window, Charlie and Ariel could see Miss Timms looking wild-eyed and distraught, speaking to a policeman and a paramedic.

'Burglary,' a man in front of them said loudly. 'They're saying someone broke into the shop while it was closed for lunch.'

'I heard Mr Cartwright surprised them,' said another, with equal confidence, 'and that's when they attacked him. They found him unconscious in the back. Weird thing is, I heard that copper saying nothing was stolen.'

'I heard they found him holding on to some box,' a lady beside him said. 'Maybe that's what they were after. You're not safe anywhere these days. It's shocking.'

Charlie felt sick.

The policewoman was moving towards them through the crowd. 'Ladies and gentlemen, we will need to speak to anyone who was in the shop today,' she said loudly, as the chatter fell away. 'Anyone who saw anything suspicious. Please, if you have any information, anything that may be useful to our enquiries, make yourself known to my colleagues over there.' She gestured towards the police car at the end of the road.

Charlie was about to open his mouth when Ariel tugged him away.

He tried to resist. 'We should tell them what we know,' he said.

'Are you mad?' she snapped. 'We'd be prime suspects. We know it wasn't us. That's enough. We can't get mixed up in all this.'

A murmur ran through the crowd as two paramedics emerged from the doorway with a stretcher. Strapped to it, wrapped tightly in a blanket, was Arnold Cartwright. A plastic oxygen mask was clamped over his nose and mouth and there was blood on his forehead. His eyes were closed. The paramedics manoeuvred the stretcher into the back of the ambulance and slammed the doors shut. Then it drove away, scattering the crowd with its siren. Gradually, people began to disperse, sensing the spectacle was over and that there was more sport to be had by sharing news of what they had seen than by standing in the cold. Kitchen tables around the town would be abuzz this evening, Charlie thought, the tale embellished with each re-telling; but he and his cousin had no appetite for gossip. Wearily, they trudged along the street towards the beach and home.

'Do you believe that crazy old guy at the museum?' Charlie asked. 'All that stuff about prison houses and poltergeists?' He looked closely at his cousin, half hoping she would dismiss it all with a shake of her head and somehow the whole terrible business would disappear. But he knew the answer that was coming as Ariel's eyes swept the incoming tide.

'Yes, I do, Charlie. Of course I do.'

Heavy clouds were rolling over the water and the light was fading fast.

Charlie tried to sound bold, summoning up some reserves of courage from within himself, but his voice faltered. 'This is the twenty-first century. Maybe that old guy is just off his head or something.'

'What does it matter which century this is? You can hear the ghost children in Darkwater. They're terrified of something. Something that's sucked the life out of poor Ferdinand and the Coopers' hens. Something that went after Cartwright in front of our eyes. Something that's still out there.' She jerked her hand back in the direction of the town as another swirl of snow gusted in on the wind and the tide surged over the sand.

Despite the cold, Charlie was glad to be out in the open. On the wide beach, you could see what was coming, what was around them: no surprises. It felt better that way. Another wave swept in, forcing them to hurry up beyond the high-tide line, scrambling onto the softer sand and stones.

And then the snow started to fall, this time heavy and sustained. Thick flakes whirled around them, draping the dunes in a coat of white. Charlie pulled up the hood of his jacket and peered out from under it in amazement: snow in London was never like this. Maybe a dusting in the park on a January morning or the occasional burst which refused to settle, but nothing so fierce as the blizzard that was now raging overhead. It was bitter against his face and lips. He felt like a figure trapped in a snow globe.

Ariel shouted over the wind, 'Let's get up onto the road. It'll be easier to walk there.'

By the time they reached it, the tarmac had already vanished under the driving snow, but they pressed on, the storm howling in off the sea. Charlie's feet were quickly wet through, the cold seeping inside his shoes. Little drifts began to pile up along the verge and etch the trees in white. The cousins slithered onwards, leaning on one another for support, while down on the beach the tide roared in, high and fast. Charlie was grateful when they reached the turn in the road and the lane that led up to Darkwater House. The snow here was already up to his ankles.

'Nearly there,' Ariel sounded relieved. 'I'm frozen.'

But as they rounded the corner, they both stopped in their tracks. Something was in the lane, half-covered by the fast-falling snow. Its eyes were open wide; its teeth bared; a dark circle of blood staining the snow around it. It had been placed so that it appeared to be staring straight at them as they approached. It was the severed head of a fox, and its body was nowhere to be seen.

Slowly, the cousins approached. Ariel crouched down in the snow beside the gruesome sight. Steam was rising faintly from the neck. She pulled off her glove and touched the fur.

'It's still warm.'

Charlie looked around at the falling snow and the white lane and dark sky. There was no one else in sight, but he had a sudden sense that something was watching them, some unseen eyes fixed upon them as they huddled together beside the macabre remains in this remote and wild place.

'I think we should get home,' he said, slowly. 'Your dad might be back if he set off early enough to beat the snow.'

The drifts were building fast beside the gateposts as they trudged up the drive. The mound of fresh earth that marked Ferdinand's grave under the apple tree had already vanished beneath the snow, which now lay thick over the lawn and clung to each crack and ledge, each tile and brick of the house, while the great trees heaved in the wind, spilling flurries of flakes around the chimney pots. There was no sign of Uncle Patrick's Land Rover, and the kitchen window was dark. They stumbled into the house, dripping wet snow over the stone floor. Only when Ariel had switched on all the lights, stoked the stove and bolted the back door, did Charlie start to feel a little calmer. He peeled off his jacket, setting it to dry on the back of a chair while his cousin brought in towels from the bathroom. Charlie started to make tea. As he waited for the kettle to boil, he watched the snow battering the windows and burying the yard.

They found the message on the answerphone some time later. The line was crackly, but the anxiety in Uncle Patrick's voice was unmistakable.

'Hi Ariel, hi Charlie. It's me. I don't know what it's like in Dunstrand, but the snow's really bad here. I packed up early, but they've already closed some of the roads and it's getting worse. The police are telling everyone to stay put. I'm really sorry, but I'm not going to make it home tonight. I'll have to find a B&B. There's plenty of food in the house, so make yourselves something to eat and I'll call you tomorrow. Take care.'

They ate beans on toast in front of the stove, its

iron door wide open. Charlie tried to look at the weather forecast on his phone, but there was no signal. A door slammed somewhere in the house. They looked at one another nervously.

'Just the wind,' Ariel said.

Charlie could see she was on edge too, which made him feel even worse. He chattered on, filling the silence. 'I was thinking. Whatever it was didn't take the box. It could have taken it after it attacked Cartwright, but it didn't. That man outside the shop said it was still in Cartwright's hands when they found him.'

'So what?'

'I just wonder whether there's something else that it's looking for. Something else that it wants.'

But before he could finish, the kitchen lights started to flicker and moments later the whole house was plunged into darkness.

'Power cut,' said Ariel. 'The lines must be down in the storm.'

Charlie's breath was coming fast and shallow. The blackness had swallowed the room, apart from a small golden square of light coming from the stove. He tried hard to focus on the dancing flames.

Ariel was quickly on her feet. 'Get the torch on your

phone. There are some candles in that cupboard.'

Charlie fumbled in his pocket and tapped the screen. The bright pinpoint of light picked out his cousin, who was already on her knees hunting around beneath the sink. She emerged with a box of candles and a couple of candlesticks. The light was feeble, but Charlie felt calmer watching the little flames grow.

'What do we do now?' he said.

Ariel frowned. 'Not much we can do. No power. Nowhere to go. I might head up to bed. You can stay down here if you want to.'

'No thanks,' said Charlie, hurriedly. 'I'm tired too.'

As they passed through the hall, Ariel lifted the phone from its cradle. It was dead. She gave a shrug as if to say it was no more than she expected, but Charlie could see the anxiety in her eyes.

In the little bathroom at the top of the house, he balanced his candle on the edge of the bath and paced about with deliberately heavy tread, splashing water nosily in the basin and humming over the whirr of his electric toothbrush to keep his wilder imaginings at bay. He dried his face and then used his towel to wipe a little peep hole in the steamed-up glass. Outside, the branches of the trees were heavy with snow and the wind lashed the dark woods beyond the garden wall.

On his way to his room, Charlie stopped outside the door where he had heard the ghost children playing. It was silent now, almost as if the children were taking refuge somewhere far away, but whether they were hiding from the storm or something worse, he did not dare imagine.

Even as he lay under the blankets, wrapped tightly in as many clothes as he could find, he could feel his fear rising along with the wind. The window frame rattled with each gust and the candle flickered on his bedside table, sending shadows of the furniture swaying over the walls. The events of the day tumbled through his mind: the swirling vortex of papers in the antique shop; the sickening crack as Cartwright struck his head; the glimpse of that dreadful face in the mirror... He turned over restlessly, thumped his pillow, flipped it round and tried to settle down again. He must have dozed off at some point because when he next awoke his phone showed it was half past one. And later, in vivid dreams, he saw tumbling snowflakes and a fox howling at the sea. The next thing he knew, he was scrabbling on the cold floor, tied up in the bedclothes while someone hammered at the door.

It took him a few seconds to come to his senses. His heart was racing as he groped about for the light on his phone. The knocking came again.

'Who is it?'

He scrambled up onto the bed.

Ariel stood in the doorway. In one hand she had a candle, in the other the hammer which they had used to open the box.

'There's someone downstairs,' she said.

'How do you know?' Charlie's voice wavered.

'I heard someone moving around. It woke me up. I want you to come down with me. We need to see who it is.'

'No way! We should stay up here. It'll be safer.'

'How do you know?' Ariel demanded. She looked him up and down with a flash of the old contempt in her eyes. 'You stay here if you want to. I'm going downstairs. If someone's in my house, I'm going to do something about it.'

She turned away and Charlie stood blinking at the empty doorway. Then, with a deep breath, he hurried after her.

'Ariel, wait for me.'

At the top of the stairs they paused. From below

there came a muffled thud. It stopped for a moment then it came again and then again. It sounded like something solid being dropped onto a wooden floor. The noise continued, resonating faster and louder around the house. Ariel's fingers drummed on the handle of the hammer and then she set off down the stairs. Charlie was so close behind he could feel the rise and fall of her ribcage as she steadied her breath.

The thudding was coming from the study at the end of the hall. The tiles were cold on Charlie's bare feet as he and his cousin positioned themselves either side of the closed door. Ariel put down the candle and raised the hammer so that its head was level with her shoulder. With her other hand, she grasped the door handle. In that instant, Charlie saw not his cousin, but a warrior: a brave and extraordinary girl who had suffered so much but who would never yield. He felt his own courage stirring.

She looked at him and nodded.

'Now!' she shouted.

They shoved open the door together and spilled inside, ready to tackle whatever might be waiting for them on the other side.

But there was nothing there.

Tentatively, Charlie waved the candle around the

room: only shadows and row upon row of empty shelves revealed themselves. Then, as he lowered his gaze, he realised the entire study was in utter disarray. Every book had been thrown onto the floor, pulled from the bookcases and hurled down by some unknown hand. They were scattered everywhere, tossed about in a jumble of spines and pages.

'Who's done this?' Charlie whispered.

Before his cousin could answer, an enormous crash came from behind them. They spun round and, as they did so, the door to the front room at the other end of the hall suddenly banged open on its hinges. Ariel set off towards it.

'This is my house,' she shouted. 'Why don't you show us who you are?'

Charlie ran after her but he had barely taken a pace over the threshold of the front room when something crunched under his feet and he stiffened with shock. The white snow outside reflected just enough light through the French windows for them to make out the Christmas tree lying full length on the floor in the centre of the room, baubles and decorations rolling loose all around. He wiped the glass fragments from the sole of his foot and felt a warm smear of blood on his fingers.

'Who's doing this?' he repeated, shouting now. 'Show us who you are!'

'Look!' Ariel was standing by the fireplace, lifting the candlestick to the mirror above it. Something had traced letters in the dusty glass: *'I shall take back what is mine. You shall all suffer as I have suffered.'*

Charlie peered at the writing in the half-light.

'What does it mean?' he whispered.

Another crash echoed loudly through the house, this time from the direction of the kitchen, and Ariel was off, running towards the noise. A single white plate lay shattered in pieces on the floor. They advanced warily, close together, eyes scanning the dark corners of the room for any sign of something lurking there. The stove glowed orange with the last embers of the fire. As they reached it there was a violent movement in the air as though the storm outside had been sucked indoors and unleashed in the heart of the house. The fire went out like a snuffed candle and then all around them the cupboard doors began to fly open, crashing back on their hinges; the drawers under the table burst out, sending knives and forks clattering across the floor; pots and pans flew from the shelves and a pile of Ariel's sketches launched themselves into the air.

Charlie heard himself scream and Ariel swung the hammer wildly. Then came a tremendous gust of wind which pushed them both hard against the wall and for a brief moment they were in the eye of the storm. A violent energy raged around them, then swept past and out into the hallway, upending the telephone table before the front door began to rattle and shake uncontrollably. The door smashed back on its hinges and, with a piercing howl, something burst out of the house and away down the driveway and into the night.

The room was silent.

Two sheets of paper from Ariel's notebook zig-zagged gently to the floor and landed at their feet. The two cousins stood there, clinging to one another, paralysed with shock like survivors of a car crash. Then, half dazed, they stumbled towards the open front door.

The blizzard was still blowing, and when they summoned the courage to peer out into the darkness, they could see, marked in the snow, a trail of human footprints snaking away over the lawn.

CHAPTER EIGHTEEN

A pale sun rose on a world transformed. The lane and wood were deep with snow and the trees in the garden sagged under the weight of their new burden. Beyond the house, the fields curved like vast white tents beneath the watery sky and the muffled silence was broken only by the sporadic cawing of a crow on the outhouse roof.

Charlie stared out of the kitchen window, hollow-eyed with fatigue. In the study he could hear Ariel picking up books and shoving them back on the shelves. They were both trying to erase the turmoil of the night before, tidying up slowly to blot out the terror and restore everyday order. But each torn page or shard of broken crockery Charlie had cleared away had dragged his mind back. He could recall each moment of the night in vivid detail: how they had bolted the front door in panic and fled to the safety of Ariel's room to barricade themselves inside, dragging the desk against the door as some primitive survival instinct kicked in. It was something neither of them now wanted nor needed to discuss. Somehow, they had endured; both crouched there in the dark, shivering with cold and shock, dozing fitfully and unable properly to sleep. At one point during the night Ariel had asked if he was awake and Charlie answered her immediately. Neither spoke again after that: it was enough simply to know that another human being was there in the house, a real human being with a beating heart and warm blood.

'What was it?' Charlie said finally, as he emptied the remains of a shattered plate into the bin. 'If you hadn't been there with me, I wouldn't have believed it. It was like...' His voice tailed off.

Ariel had come into the kitchen and was gathering scattered saucepans from the floor. 'It was a poltergeist. Malicious. Vicious. The old man was right; it should have been left alone.'

'Bit late for that.'

They revived themselves with hot chocolate and found the energy to put the Christmas tree back in its place and wipe the writing from the mirror.

'*I shall take back what is mine,*' Ariel read, as she

rubbed out the letters with a cloth. 'It's still looking for something. That's why it was turning the place upside down.'

'And the bit about suffering?' Charlie asked.

'It's like the old man said. It's angry. It's been locked up for years and now no one in the whole town is safe from it.'

'But maybe it will leave *us* alone now. It found nothing here last night.'

Ariel thought for a moment. 'What about that tiny little medallion that was in the box? What did you do with that?'

'I gave it to the horse.'

Ariel stared at him in surprise. 'What did you do that for?'

'I sort of wanted to...thank him. It was that night when we were decorating the tree. You had that argument with your dad, so I went out to Bobby's stable box and I just sort of hung out with him for a bit.'

The clock in the hallway chimed the hour.

'The Christmas concert!' Ariel said suddenly. 'I'd completely forgotten! It's this morning. Come on! We've got to get going.'

They pulled on their boots and hurried out into

the cold. It was heavy going down the lane through the deep drifts. The crunch of their feet and the panting of their breath were the only sounds as they slithered towards the beach where the waves had wiped the shore of snow and walking was easier, but it was another half an hour before they made it to town. As they approached the church hall, its roof domed white like an igloo, they could hear voices raised in animated conversation and found Miss Stanford talking earnestly with a group of parents.

'I'm glad you two have made it through,' she said, looking relieved to see them. 'But the main road into Dunstrand is blocked. That means many of our parents and children can't make it in, so I think we shall have to cancel. It's such a dreadful shame after everyone has worked so hard.'

'Has the church hall got power?'

She nodded. 'Most of Dunstrand is back on, but lots of places around are still off. It could be hours.'

'We must do the performance. If we have power, then we can,' said Ariel firmly.

'But, Ariel, the road is—'

The noise of an engine interrupted them. At the top of the street, the farm tractor was edging towards them with David Cooper at the wheel and

William and Rose beaming in delight beside him. The tractor's shovel was lowered to act as an improvised snow plough and it was clearing the way as it went.

'Good morning!' David said as he leaned out of the window. 'I'll get to work on the main road if you can keep an eye on these two.'

He opened the door and helped his children onto the little folding step beside the cab, from which Charlie swung them down gently to the ground. They each grabbed his hand and began to bounce up and down, giggling with delight.

'Thank you, Charlie. They will keep you busy, I promise. Now, I reckon I can get things opened up in a half an hour or so. Someone had better do a ring-round and let the other parents know. Takes more than a bit of snow to stop us round here.'

The tractor backed up and lurched off towards the coast road with another blast of its horn, and Charlie followed Ariel inside the hall. Once they had removed their wet boots, leaving them in an icy puddle in the entrance, they began to help Miss Stanford set up the props for the opening of the show. They worked away busily, grateful to have something new to occupy their thoughts. Mr Brooke the pianist was next to arrive, proudly wearing an ancient pair of snowshoes.

'It's a couple of feet deep on my side of town,' he said, peeling off his gloves and flexing his finger. 'And more in the drifts. We haven't had a storm like it in years. What a wild night! There were even a couple of windows smashed down at the museum.'

Before Charlie could ask him anything further, the first excited shrieks of the children began to roll through the hall and William and Rose ran to greet the new arrivals.

Miss Stanford beamed. 'It looks like some people are starting to make it through. Mr Brooke, there's a contact sheet in that folder on the piano. I would be grateful if you could start calling the parents to let them know the road will be open and that we will be going ahead as soon as we can.' Turning back to the arriving children, she said: 'Come on in everyone. Leave your boots at the back.'

The pile of coats and scarves in the entrance hall grew, and the air filled with stories of the struggle into town. Eventually, and only a little later than planned, the audience settled into the red plastic chairs and Charlie helped Miss Stanford herd the children towards their starting places backstage. Mr Brooke struck up the first bars of the opening number and the Christmas concert began.

Charlie watched from the wings. He could see the children singing in profile and Ariel looking across at him from the opposite side of the stage. Her face was pale, with dark circles under her eyes; he supposed he looked no better. He gave her an encouraging thumbs-up and she smiled. Charlie could see Clara Cooper in the second row, her eyes closed and her head back, listening to the music with a peaceful expression on her face. David and his wife sat beside her, watching eagerly as William and Rose sang with enthusiasm. Miss Stanford's face shone with pride.

As the show moved towards the finale, the children gathered in a group at the front of the stage. Charlie rubbed his eyes and yawned. He suddenly felt light-headed with fatigue and rocked his head from side to side to ease the stiffness in his neck and shoulders. Through the side window of the hall, he could see thick snow lying on the roofs of the town; the children's singing grew louder, the piano more vigorous, as Charlie yawned again. Then, for a brief moment, he thought he saw something flicker like a shadow across the dazzling whiteness outside. He shook his head. His eyelids felt unnaturally heavy. Turning back into the hall, he could see Ariel following Miss Stanford's hands as they beat in time to the music.

The door at the back of the hall swung open. Someone in the last row got up to close it as a chill breeze blew in, but nobody else seemed to notice: they had eyes and ears only for the performance. A faint draught stirred the programmes on the table by the far wall and a couple of them fluttered to the floor. A lady on the aisle pulled her coat more tightly around her. The singing went on. Mr Brooke's fingers moved over the keys. Miss Stanford conducted the singing. The children's eyes followed the movement of her hands.

Suddenly Charlie felt the temperature plummet around him and he was gripped by an icy cold, as if he had stepped inside a refrigerator. And then came a peculiar sensation as if he were standing outside the hall rather than in it and the whole scene was a picture painted on a Christmas card that he was holding in his hands. He felt suddenly able to observe everything around him while everyone else was frozen in their own world. It seemed as if the singing had stopped and the children were mouthing their words in silence.

The set shook slightly. Then Charlie noticed something that chilled him to the core.

One of the heavy stage lights on the rig above

the children's heads was starting to shake. Gently at first, then faster and faster, making it rattle and judder. Now the big chrome bolts which held the lamp in place started to turn as if some imperceptible, immensely strong hand were twisting them. Below, the children's mouths moved silently. Mr Brooke's hands travelled noiselessly over the keys. Miss Stanford conducted a dumb show. The lamp began to shudder.

'Look out!'

Everything seemed to happen in slow motion after that.

After his shout, Charlie leapt out from the side of the stage and hurled himself forward. He dived full length and shoved Rose Cooper to one side like a rugby player making a tackle, just as the heavy lamp crashed down from the rig above and smashed onto the stage. Someone screamed and the world suddenly sped up in a tumult of raised voices and shouts. There was pandemonium in the hall as people rushed onto the stage. Amid the mayhem a single child's voice rose in a wail above the chaos.

Ariel was beside him, helping him sit up. 'Are you OK, Charlie?'

'I think so.'

A crowd of parents and frightened children surged around him. Among the feet and the legs and the noise, he saw the broken light and Rose Cooper beside it, her face as white as the snow outside while her mother cradled her in her arms. Then David was there too, shoving everyone aside to create a space for his family. Someone shouted for an ambulance. The audience were out of their seats, swarming round the hall.

Ariel helped Charlie to his feet. 'You saved her.'

The shouts and wails grew louder. One of the parents was standing on a chair appealing for calm. Miss Stanford was being comforted by Mr Brooke. Children were in tears, bewildered by the accident, and it was many minutes before order was restored. Someone had found a blanket by then and had draped it over Rose's shoulders. Her father lifted her up gently in his arms and hurried away with her over his shoulder. Charlie and Ariel sat on the edge of the scene, stunned by what they had witnessed.

'She'll be all right, thanks to you Charlie,' said Mr Brooke, 'but what a terrible accident! Awful! Awful!' He went away, shaking his head.

'It wasn't an accident, you know.' Charlie whispered to Ariel.

'What do you mean?'

'It came into the hall. It was here again. It was like I could feel it was there and could sense what it was about to do. That's how I was able to move over so fast and get Rose out of the way.'

He looked at his cousin with something near to despair etched in his eyes.

'Ariel, what are we going to do? It's dangerous and it's going to make everyone suffer like it promised. It nearly killed Rose. It's getting stronger and it's not going to go away. We've done this, Ariel. This is all our fault.'

Someone called his name.

Clara Cooper was moving slowly towards them, Pebble guiding her through the dispersing crowd.

'Thank you, Charlie. I understand you saved my granddaughter. We are all very grateful.'

He shifted uncomfortably from foot to foot.

'What's the matter?' she asked. 'You seem...pre-occupied. Both of you.'

'I just think it's the shock,' Ariel said.

Clara tilted her head slowly to one side and Charlie had that strange feeling again that she was peering into his thoughts.

'I cannot shake the sense that you two have

something grave on your minds,' she said. 'Something that is causing you both a great deal of anxiety. That makes me think it is something out of the ordinary, something which you do not wish to share. In which case, if I am right, I can only advise you to seek the help of Dr Ellison.'

'Who's he?' asked Ariel.

'Oh, he has lived around here for almost as long as I have and brought half the district into the world in his time. You will find his cottage on the other side of the headland, past all the others. He will know what to do. He knows more than you would think about' – she paused as if searching for the right words – 'unusual events.' She leaned closer and rested her hand lightly on Ariel's arm. 'After what has happened here today,' she whispered, 'I can assure you this is no longer a game.'

Someone called Clara's name from the back of the hall.

'I must be going,' the old lady said. 'Remember: Dr Ellison.'

Pebble pulled at his harness and led her away.

'What was that all about?' said Charlie. 'What do you think she knows?'

Ariel shrugged. 'Her intuition is good. Let's hope this Dr Ellison is too.'

CHAPTER NINETEEN

The cottage stood a little way apart from the rest, well beyond the lighthouse and headland, as if whoever had built it years ago wanted to distance himself from his neighbours, but without quite abandoning society entirely. Dunstrand was at the cousins' backs, and out to sea dark clouds were moving inland; it felt as if it would snow again before evening. The garden was dominated by a pine tree, bent to one side by the wind. The curtains at the front windows were drawn tight and there was a sniff of coal smoke in the air. Ariel took off her glove and banged on the door three times.

'What if he's not here?' Charlie whispered.

Faint stirrings came from within.

'Wait a minute!' The voice sounded annoyed at the disturbance. There were footsteps in the hall and the sound of a bolt being drawn, before the door swung slowly open. Charlie let out a gasp.

Standing in front of them was the same bright-eyed old man whom they had met in the museum the day before and who had warned him about the box on that very first day. He wore a dark velvet dressing gown and his face was solemn.

'Well, well. Look who is here. The two children who ignored my advice and then lied to me about what they had done. You are very foolish. I had hoped for better, but I am not surprised.'

'I'm sorry,' Charlie blurted out. 'How did you know?'

Dr Ellison ran a hand through his hair. 'This is a quiet place,' he said slowly, 'and yet this morning I hear on the wireless news of a break-in at the antique shop and the owner left fighting for his life. The newspaper boy was full of chatter about smashed windows at the museum, and the talk in the Mariner's Arms is of livestock killed on surrounding farms. Something is clearly amiss.' He pointed an accusing finger directly at Charlie. 'I told you. And you did not listen.'

The words fell heavily in the cold air.

Ariel broke the silence. 'Clara Cooper said you could help us.'

'Oh, did she?' There was a faint note of sarcasm

in his reply. 'She is a fine lady but mistaken on this occasion. I cannot help you.'

'Can't? Or won't?'

'Young lady, last week I celebrated my eighty-fourth birthday. I have neither the energy nor the inclination to clear up the mess that you two have created.'

'Then why did Clara say you could help us? She said you knew about these sorts of things.'

Dr Ellison's hand tightened into a fist. 'That is nothing more than small-town tittle-tattle! Slander even. I am – I *was* – the local doctor here for many years. My trade is science not superstition. Now I suggest you two run along and play in the snow. Build a snowman, if that's what young people still do these days. There's nothing I can do to help you with the problem that you have created.'

And with that, he slammed the door shut.

The two children looked at one another.

'Miserable old man,' said Ariel. 'What a waste of time coming out here.'

Charlie chewed his lip. Something was bothering him. Something he had seen over the old man's shoulder as he had stood in the doorway. He closed his eyes for a moment, trying to remember: on the table in the hall...a bowl of keys and a hat, and above them a picture on the wall... It was a screen print, with big, bold black letters that looked like part of a quotation. He screwed his eyes tighter... It had said: '*All the devils...*'

Charlie hammered on the door.

'What are you doing?'

Ignoring his cousin, he flipped up the letterbox and shouted through it at the top of his voice. 'Dr Ellison! Dr Ellison! What are you hiding from us? I've seen the words in that picture on your wall. You know way more than you're telling us. You knew about that painting in the museum. You knew about the box. You can't just turn your back on everything now because you're angry with us. There are two people in hospital because of all this and someone will get killed if it carries on. You might be too old to care about stopping it, but we're not. When did you stop caring, Dr Ellison? I thought caring was what doctors were supposed to do?'

His words rang down the empty hall. When no reply came, he pressed his forehead to the letterbox and strained his eyes to search deeper into the gloom inside. Was that the old man, standing stock-still at the back of the house, his head bowed? He could not be certain. He shouted again: 'Well we care, Dr Ellison. My cousin and I care very much. We know we made a big mistake opening that box, but we're going to put it right – with or without your help.'

The shape in the darkness did not move.

'Please help us, Dr Ellison. Please.'

But no answer came.

———◇———

They passed a café in the market square with Christmas lights hung in the window and a basket of thick-crusted mince pies beneath. Charlie felt a sudden pang of hunger and realised they had missed lunch. Remembering the last few pounds he had left from the money his mother had given him, he said: 'I need to eat.'

Inside the café, the air smelled of damp coats and coffee. A harassed-looking waitress pushed her way between crowded aisles and nodded at a spare table in the window. Condensation trickled down the glass, blurring the view of the Mariner's Arms opposite as if they were looking at it through the porthole of a ship in a storm. They ordered hot chocolate and thick slabs of Christmas cake and devoured them, ravenous.

'So, it's just us now,' Ariel said. 'We have to get rid of this…thing.'

'How?'

'I think we have to draw it out into the open. We need to meet it on our terms, not let it ambush us again.'

'And if we do, what then?'

'We need to ask it exactly what it wants.'

'You're suggesting we talk to it? You make it sound like we're dealing with something normal! You're crazy, Ariel. The thing has gone wild any time it has been anywhere near us. It's dangerous. Look what it did to Cartwright and Rose Cooper. What did Dr Ellison say at the museum yesterday? It's evil. It's angry.'

'But what if we set the terms? What if we lure it somewhere where we have the upper hand for a change?'

Charlie sucked the froth from his drink. 'How would we do that?'

'We lie. We tell it we have got what it's looking for.'

'How do we do that? Send it a text?'

'We could tell it, next time it appears. It can communicate, because it wrote that stuff on the mirror. And it will be back, I'm certain.'

Charlie wiped the window with his finger. Outside, a group of people in uniform were gathering around the Christmas tree in the square. Some of them began to pull brass instruments from cases they had set down in the snow.

'The Salvation Army,' said Charlie, distracted. 'They've got a hall at the end of our road.'

The strains of 'Good King Wenceslas' began to drift across the marketplace and the hubbub inside the cafe subsided as everyone turned to listen. As the band played, Charlie felt the food and the hot chocolate warming his tired body. Then, gradually, the chatter around them resumed. He finished his drink and let out a laugh.

'What is it?'

He shook his head. 'All this! Everything we've been talking about today. What are we thinking? We've lost the plot! A poltergeist? I'll be back in London in a couple of days and I can just leave all this behind.'

Ariel looked at him, shocked. 'You're joking, aren't you? You can't just walk away. What about me? I'll still be here in two days' time cleaning up the chaos you've created.'

'I've created? Hang on a minute. It was you who decided to open the box. I was always going to chuck it back in the sea until you—'

But Ariel had already pushed back her chair and had stomped off to the toilets at the back of the café. Charlie threw his spoon across the table in frustration. He could see why his uncle lost his temper with her sometimes.

Outside, a small crowd had gathered around the Salvation Army band. Charlie watched them for a moment through the window as a breeze started to ruffle the lights on the tree. Then the music sheets of the singers began to shake, gently at first as if tugged by an invisible hand. Charlie put down his mug, feeling the adrenaline rise. Then the Christmas tree itself started to sway and suddenly puffs of snow began to curl around the legs of the singers, turning on the wind. A bike in the cycle rack clattered to the ground.

Charlie got up, threw some change onto the table and ran out into the street. The cold air snapped in his face and, in his haste, he slipped on the icy road. 'Look out!' he managed to shout at the singers, but he was already tumbling to the ground and his warning was lost in the snowy cobbles.

In any case, it was too late. A powerful gale whipped around the square and there was an eruption of snowflakes as the the tree shook violently. Someone screamed. Sheets of music flew high into the air. In the confusion, Charlie found himself looking up at people scattering in all directions, shouting and shrieking. He tried to struggle to his feet, but he slipped again and then watched in horror as a footprint appeared in the fresh snow in front of him. Then another. And another. For a fleeting moment, he thought he could see the faint outline of a boot flashing by, like a flicker in a mirror. The footprints were heading across the square. Charlie scrambled to his feet and followed the tracks, which abruptly switched direction down the alleyway beside the Mariner's Arms. Sliding over the snow, Charlie gave chase, skidding to a halt beneath a single lamp post, where he hesitated, peering into the gloom ahead. He could see nothing except for a couple of wheelie bins full of empty bottles by the back gate of the pub. Cautiously, he took two paces forward.

'I know you're here,' he said, his voice wavering at first, then growing stronger. 'But you can't stay in this town. You don't belong here.'

His words echoed off the walls and sounded

unnaturally loud in his ears.

'You've hurt people. You've got to stop.'

A whisper of snow stirred in the shadows.

'Whatever it is you want, we can help. But you have to tell us what you are looking for. And you have to promise to stop all this.'

Emboldened, Charlie walked on slowly down the alley with deliberate, measured strides. His voice was soothing.

'Just promise me that you won't hurt anyone else.'

There was a rustling in front of him, as if someone had stood up. Then, just ahead, the outline of a man emerged from the shadows. Charlie's feet faltered and his throat tightened. He wanted to turn away but found himself transfixed by the apparition's hollow gaze. The figure was tall and broad with the same blistered skin that Charlie had glimpsed before. The stare that now held him was coming from two dark sockets set in a burnt and scarred face. The man's clothes were rough: a tattered jerkin, ragged trousers and split boots. His great hands hung by his sides, the fingers twisted like claws. But most extraordinary of all was that he seemed to be translucent, almost as if his body had been carved from ice. He was there and not there at the same time. Charlie could see the brickwork of the alley wall right through him.

'Who are you?' he whispered.

Slowly, the figure stretched out its hand towards Charlie, the palm facing up to the sky.

'I don't understand...' Charlie's voice faltered.

At that moment, Ariel came hurtling around the corner.

'Charlie!' she shouted. 'Look out!'

The noise had an instant effect on the figure at the end of the alley. It sprang towards Charlie, who stood frozen with fear. And then it was upon him, the blank eyes and twisted hands up close. He had a sudden sensation of being enveloped in a violent grip of fury and anger. It broke all around him like a wave before a huge physical force smashed him off his feet, sending him spinning into the wall and down into the snow.

'Charlie!'

Then Ariel, too, was knocked sideways and there was a huge crash as one of the bins tipped forward, spewing glass over the snow. The figure vanished among the shadows once more and then two, three, four bottles went flying through the air, before smashing in a rapid volley against the wall above Charlie's head. In the snow in front of him he saw footprints racing back towards the square.

Ariel rolled over and groaned, blood trickling from her lip. She struggled to her feet and staggered down the alley to her cousin, helping him sit up. Half his face was caked in snow and there was blood seeping from his nose. It took a few seconds for him to realise where he was.

'Are you OK?' she asked.

'My head hurts.'

'Try and get up.' Ariel put her arm round his shoulder and leant back against the wall. They sat together for a moment, shivering in the lamplight.

'Did you see it?' he said.

Ariel nodded.

He grimaced. 'I don't think we're going to be able to reason with it, Ariel.'

'Sorry. Bad idea.'

A shadow fell over them and for an instant they clung together tighter, fearing the worst. Then they heard a familiar voice: 'It seems I owe you both an apology – and an explanation. I have underestimated not only your determination but also your courage. I think you had both better come back with me.'

They looked up from the ground. There, leaning on his stick, was Dr Ellison.

CHAPTER TWENTY

The light was so bright it hurt, but Charlie could not blink because someone was holding his eyelids firmly apart. The beam moved in slow circles before his eyes and the voice behind it was deep and soothing. He felt calm and quite content to sit in a state of suspended reality, watching the light, listening to the voice.

'It all looks as it should,' Dr Ellison said gently. 'No lasting damage, but I suspect that bruise will be spectacular.'

He snapped off his torch.

They were sitting in the cramped kitchen of Dr Ellison's cottage, bread and cheese on the table beside a battered old medical bag. Ariel was chewing thoughtfully, her eyes fixed on the doctor as he packed away his torch and stethoscope.

'You said you'd explain,' she said.

'And I will, now we have established young Charlie is fit to fight another day.'

He poured three cups of tea from the pot and carried them on a tin tray to the study next door. One wall was entirely filled with books: old medical journals lined the shelves, interspersed with well-thumbed paperbacks and files overflowing with papers. Under the window, the legs of an antique desk were just visible beneath piles of newspapers and magazines. On the mantelpiece, a youthful-looking Dr Ellison stared out rather awkwardly from a photograph, dressed in a white medical coat. In another, grey and bearded, he leaned happily against the tiller of a yacht at sea. A fire burned low in the grate beside two high-backed armchairs and the room carried the faint scent of cigar smoke. Dr Ellison stoked the fire and the three of them sat down, watching for a moment as the flames caught the fresh coals.

Ariel broke the silence. 'So, what have you got to tell us?' she said.

Dr Ellison nodded towards an alcove in the corner of the room which was screened by a velvet curtain. 'Take a look behind there. No need to be frightened. I can assure you, it's perfectly safe.'

Tentatively, Charlie drew the curtain back to reveal a heavy sea chest, the type that might have accompanied a wealthy Victorian traveller to some far-flung land.

'Pull it over here.'

With some effort, Charlie dragged the chest in front of the fire.

'Open it.'

It took a moment for Charlie's fingers to work the catch. Once he had got it open, he lifted the lid and let out a little cry of surprise. Sitting on top of a pile of papers and leather journals were seven brass boxes, bright and polished. Each had the same design carved into the lid: a tree with spreading branches and a split trunk, inside which a tiny prisoner screamed silent agony and beside it the familiar words: 'All the devils are here...' The boxes all looked so new, they might have been made that morning. With some effort, Dr Ellison leaned forward and picked one up.

'The boxes of souls,' he said quietly. 'This is the only surviving collection of them. Long since gone from this world. They are the last. Apart from, it seems, the one you stumbled upon a few days ago.'

'Box of souls? What's that?'

'I am not certain you properly understood me

when I saw you both in the reading room at the museum yesterday. Perhaps, in my frustration and agitation, I was not making myself clear. For that I am sorry.

'A box of souls is a container for the spirits of the dead. A place to capture and preserve them: a prison house for those souls who cannot – or will not – leave this world when their time is done. It is believed the boxes were first used by the Ancient Egyptians and Greeks, then again in certain parts of Asia and the Middle East. Nobody seems quite sure, and even fewer people really knew how to use them. Apart from my great-grandfather.'

The children looked bewildered.

'What I am about to tell you,' Dr Ellison said, settling back in his chair, 'I have never told anyone else before. But you two are now so deep into this business that I believe you have a right to know. I have seen for myself your courage and determination and I am at a time of my life when my stocks of both are diminishing. I shall not see the Christmas season many more times and someone else must know my secret. I have no children of my own and you two are the right people to hear it, I think. There was a time when what I am about to share with you would have been enough to finish my career as a medical practitioner. They would have thrown me out and called me a crank, but I am now at a point in my life where I do not think there is any reason to hide the truth any longer.'

He sat silent for a moment. The fire crackled. Outside, the wind blew a flurry of snow against the glass.

'My great-grandfather was called Tobias Ellison and he was an unusual young man. He saw the world differently, for good or ill. He studied medicine at Edinburgh, but was dismissed from the university, partly for his wild behaviour and partly for neglecting his studies. It wasn't that he was lazy – far from it – it was just that he had an eye for the bizarre and an insatiable curiosity for the... less conventional branches of medicine. In particular he was fascinated by the power of the mind and he developed theories about extra-sensory perception, the sort of sixth sense some people have before a moment of danger, or the way in which twins know something has happened to each other, despite their being miles apart. He became fascinated by the idea of telepathy and hypnosis and was heavily influenced by the seances which so infused Victorian culture.

None of which, of course, endeared him to the medical establishment of the day or the university authorities.'

The children sat watching the old man intently. He took a sip of his tea and continued.

'And so, Tobias went his own way. There was some family money in those days and off he went, travelling the world searching for the knowledge and insights to complete his studies in his own unique fashion. There's a photograph of him in there.'

He pointed towards the upturned lid of the trunk and Ariel pulled out a faded picture, blurred with age and dotted with ink spots. It showed a tall, slim man dressed in a long black coat. His hair was swept back down to his collar and he stared at the camera with a wry smile on his lips as if not taking the novel process of having his photograph taken entirely seriously.

'And so Tobias travelled. He was away for seven years. Most of the family thought he was dead. He spent time in Egypt, Greece and then India, where he lived with the fakirs of Delhi for many months. Elsewhere in Asia, he studied with monks and learned to meditate, and he travelled the ancient Silk Road through the markets and bazaars of China and when he finally returned to London, his own unique education was complete. And among the many macabre and peculiar objects that he shipped back to England were these.'

He lifted the brass box up again and held it to the light. 'The boxes of souls.'

Charlie felt a tingle of electricity run down his spine.

'What happened after that?'

'Not long after his return, Tobias was contacted by a wealthy landowner. The man had an unusual problem that nobody had been able to solve. He had recently bought a couple of large farms in the north of England after the bankruptcy and suicide of the original owner. But not long after he had done so, the crops began to wither in the fields, with no apparent explanation. Cattle grew sick and the harvest failed. The farm workers were convinced that the original owner had put a curse on the place, and the talk in the neighbourhood was of his malevolent spirit stalking the district. Two young men claimed to have seen a strange figure walking the fields at night, and wild tales raged around.

'The new owner was at his wits' end. His workers were leaving. His investment was in tatters and he faced ruin. He was discussing this strange story over dinner one night, when one of the assembled company mentioned the name of Tobias Ellison. It was suggested that my great-grandfather was just the sort of fellow who would relish the opportunity to tackle such a peculiar challenge. He was certainly the only man in England who would have any idea where to start.'

'What happened?' Ariel asked.

'The landowner wrote to Tobias, who travelled north immediately, setting himself up in the village inn, equipped with his notebooks and various artefacts from his travels, including one of these boxes. A week later Tobias was found lying in a field outside the farmhouse, his clothes shredded and his face bloodied and with, by all accounts, a manic smile on his face. He had the box gripped tightly to his chest. All he would say to the landowner was that the man's problems were now at an end. And so it proved. The hauntings and sightings stopped, the crops flourished and the farm returned to profit. Tobias' reputation soared. Word got around, you see. Here was a talented, if eccentric, young man who could make the most unusual problems disappear.

'From all over Europe the letters came flooding in: a case of possession in an eminent Italian family;

a wealthy Athenian haunted by the ghost of a long-dead servant... Poltergeists, spirits, even an outbreak of vampirism in the Balkans... Soon Tobias Ellison had more work that he could handle alone.'

'So what did he do?' asked Charlie.

'He got help. And a rum crew they were too, but his line of work tended to attract the unconventional: a fortune-teller; a lapsed priest; a German medical student who had written a radical paper on the power of hypnosis. Together they made up a discreet network across the continent, all run from Tobias' rooms in London. They called themselves the Cloven Pine, a society that specialised in dealing with what you might call...paranormal problems.'

'And you have that screen print of their motto framed in your hallway,' said Charlie.

'You are an observant young man.'

'It's a Shakespeare quotation,' said Ariel.

'Very good,' Dr Ellison nodded. 'Tobias Ellison had the mind of a scientist but the soul of a poet. The idea of the cloven pine tree as an enchanted trap and the line about the devils were lifted straight from *The Tempest*. They provided his new society with just the sort of flamboyant touch he enjoyed. A few months earlier, he had fallen in love with a young actress who soon became his wife and mother to his son. I've no doubt she encouraged his Shakespearean flourishes. And no doubt it was good for business too. A touch of the fantastic.'

Ariel leaned forward in her chair. 'This is a good story, but how does any of it help us?'

For a moment a spark seemed to flicker in the old man's eyes, as if some distant memory was stirring in the recesses of his brain.

'I am coming to that. Perhaps it will not surprise you to learn, given the strange life my great-grandfather led, that he died at a young age. Only thirty-three years old.'

'What happened to him?'

'You saw the picture in the museum. He drowned. Out there.'

Dr Ellison raised himself to his feet and drew back the curtains. Beyond the snowy garden, the bell-buoy's light marking the Serpent's Tongue rocks blinked on the black sea.

'In the winter of 1897, he was returning from Europe on a small passenger steamer, the *Miranda*. According to eye-witness accounts, it was driven onto the sandbanks off the headland and broke up just as the Dunstrand lifeboat reached it. Many lives were lost. But those who survived talked afterwards of a man, matching my great-grandfather's description, who helped save them. And they said he threw something – his travelling case most likely – very deliberately into the water just as the boat was destroyed by the sea.

'That was Tobias' final act of heroism. Heaven knows what dreadful objects the case contained, but I have no doubt the box of souls which you found buried in the sand was one of them. I am certain that by casting his travelling case deep into the sea, my great-grandfather was doing his best to drown the devils he had captured and save this town from what was inside.'

They sat in silence for a moment. A coal fell in the grate and orange sparks spiralled up the chimney breast. Dr Ellison eased himself back in his chair, finished his tea and began to speak again.

'In the decades that followed, lurid legends grew up around the mysterious passenger and his cargo on board that ship. Chancers like Arnold Cartwright have been on the look-out for that cargo for years, but nobody ever knew the real story and no one has ever found anything. Not the beachcombers nor the fishermen nor the walkers on the shore; nobody for over a hundred years, until you, Charlie. Until you.'

'Why didn't you tell me this before?' said Charlie. 'You saw me with the box in the antique shop that day and you said nothing.'

'I warned you. I told you to throw the box of souls straight back into the sea. I knew it would bring only trouble to this town and so it has proved. Even after all this time there are some things that are best left undisturbed.'

'Well, you were right. We did open it,' Charlie said quietly, 'and I wish we hadn't. And now we don't even have it any more. It was stolen.' His eyes filled with tears and the story of the past few days spilled out.

He told the doctor everything: from first hearing the ghostly children's voices at Darkwater House to searching the beach with the metal detector. He spoke of Cartwright's obsession with the box and how they had smashed it open in the attic room only for the antique dealer to steal it from them. He told of the strange deaths of creatures around the house and farm, the attack on Cartwright in his own shop, the night of horror at the house in the storm and then finally the near-fatal incident at the Christmas concert.

Dr Ellison sat impassive throughout, staring into the fire. He continued to sit in silence long after Charlie had finished.

'Tell me one thing,' he said finally. 'Is it just you two who can hear the voices of the ghost children in Darkwater House? No one else?'

'No one else.'

'Fascinating! Tobias' journals talk of the very few among us who can tune in to hear the voices of those long dead. The echoes in the shadows, he calls them. It is a rare and special power that may be of great use to us if we are to bring this dreadful business to a conclusion. He could do it, but why you two as well, I wonder? Why here and why now?'

Ariel shook her head. 'We've told you our story, Dr Ellison. Why have you never told anyone yours?'

The old man spread his hands defensively and when he spoke it was slowly, choosing his words with great care.

'I have been a doctor in these parts for many, many years and I have been fortunate to keep a house on the coast. Sailing was always my thing you see,' he gestured at the picture on the mantelpiece. 'When I retired, I continued to work part-time as a GP here, helping out when I was needed. My reputation was as a man of medicine, of science. A pillar of the community, you might say. I did not want to be known as the local crackpot.'

'But someone did know, didn't they?' Ariel said sharply. 'Clara Cooper told us that you knew all about this sort of stuff.'

Dr Ellison sighed and bowed his head. 'She did know something of my secret interest in...the unconventional.'

'How?'

'Many, many years ago I treated one of her sisters, Elsie. She was pale, fainting, barely able to get out of bed, and no doctor in the county had been able to diagnose her condition, let alone cure it. Her family even took her to see a specialist in London, but nothing worked. They were in despair and it looked as if the end would come quickly, which was when I wondered if I could take a leaf out of my great-grandfather's book. Literally.' He waved his hand towards the piles of journals in the trunk. 'Once, in India, Tobias witnessed the exorcism of an evil spirit that had entered the body of a young girl, the daughter of a politician and a wealthy man. As a last resort, I decided to try the same technique to help Elsie Cooper. To my utter astonishment, it worked.'

'What happened after that?'

'I swore Clara to secrecy. To tell you the truth, I was frightened. I had read enough of Tobias' journals to know that not everyone has the power to operate in that way. Tobias believed some people were more naturally attuned to the spirit world than others, innately better able to connect with it through a mixture of their own experiences and the make-up of their minds. Clara believed that too, but I didn't want anything to do with it. It flew in the face of everything I had studied, all the science I had learned. So I shut it all out.'

'And that was it?'

'Not quite,' Dr Ellison looked ashamed. 'I was curious, of course. And eventually my curiosity got the better of me. I was reading my great-grandfather's journals in secret and after a while I was tempted to create a potion he had once concocted in Asia. It was made of herbs and spices and he had used it to treat the infected wound of an old man. I tried it on one of my patients here, and again it worked where traditional medicine had failed. After that, word got around the practice and some of the medical authorities were unimpressed. Quackery, they called it. So I stopped. But it made me realise there is much in this world we do not understand, no matter how smart and sophisticated we believe ourselves to be. It is wise to keep an open mind on all things – including this little problem we have in front of us now.'

'So how do we solve it?' Charlie asked.

'I suspect the key to this business is to understand what we are up against. My great-grandfather's methods owed a lot to the idea of knowing your enemy.' Dr Ellison leaned forward and sifted through a pile of papers in the trunk. 'In this case, I think we are safe to suppose that he had captured something in that particular box of souls you found, Charlie – something that was so strong and aggressive it needed to be imprisoned permanently. Most likely a poltergeist of some sort, a violent spirit with a tendency to vampirism, as your poor cat would testify, if it were in any position to do so.'

There was a sudden thump at the window that made the children jump nervously.

'Snow, falling from the roof,' said the doctor, peering out.

'Are all these journals written by Tobias Ellison?' asked Charlie, opening a book full of tiny, spidery handwriting.

'Yes. They are the notes he kept throughout his

studies and travels.'

'What about these?' Charlie lifted out a stack of papers. 'These have different handwriting.'

'They are some of the letters that were sent to him and the society. People asking for help.'

'And where did you say he had been before he died?'

'The continent. January 1897 was when his ship was wrecked.'

Charlie said slowly, 'So presumably someone had written to Tobias from Europe a little before that date asking for his help? He had been abroad responding to a request. If we could find a letter with the right date, then we would know what he had been doing and what he eventually brought back inside the box of souls.'

Dr Ellison nodded slowly. He instructed the children to remove two thick sheaves of letters from the trunk while he swept his desk clear, sending papers spinning to the floor. 'Most of these I have catalogued over the years. Now let us see…'

The children helped him spread the letters out under the lamplight while he flitted over each with a magnifying glass. After several minutes of peering and squinting, he pulled a couple of faded yellow papers from the pile.

'The date is right,' he said excitedly. 'I think this may well be the one. My eyes are bad for this sort of thing. Here, Ariel, take it. Read it aloud to us now.'

CHAPTER TWENTY-ONE

12th November 1896,
Amsterdam

Dear Mr Ellison,

Forgive my writing to you without formal introduction. I expect you receive many such letters, but it is my hope that what I am about to set out before you in these pages will be of interest to a man of your unusual talents.

For much of my youth I studied and worked in England, eventually mastering your language and learning the many customs of your island, and it was through a business acquaintance of mine in the county of Kent that I first heard mention of your name. I now write to you to beg for your help with a terrible problem which threatens to overwhelm me. Let me set out the facts.

My family is in the business of importing and exporting

goods through the port of Amsterdam: mostly wool, silks and cloth. Over the years, we have made a success of our trade through diligence and hard work and, when my father died two years ago, I was honoured to take on his role at the head of the family business.

Like most sons in my position, I had plans to improve and expand our interests and was quick to acquire an additional warehouse on the banks of the River Amstel, a few hundred yards away from our office. The investment was substantial, but the long-term returns favourable. However, the first inkling of the difficulties that lay ahead appeared just a month into our new venture.

Boats were in and out of the port all the time and each month we used to land a cargo of textiles from England. It was the same ship that made the passage each time, the Prosperous, *under the command of a particularly loathsome captain. His name was Jack Raven and he was feared by all who knew him. Quick-tempered, violent and fond of drink, he was a big man who used his great size and strength to intimidate those around him. He had few friends among the dockers and workers: his reputation was as an experienced sailor but also as an unscrupulous bully.*

Once his cargo was unloaded, Raven liked nothing more than to drink in the taverns along the dockside and to gamble at cards or dice. Rumour had it he had once killed a man in a fight, sending the poor fellow to the bottom of the Amstel with a single blow of his fist.

But let me stick to the facts of my case.

One spring night, when the tulips were in bloom, a young man in my employ joined a card game in one of the taverns close to our new warehouse. Jan Kopek was bright and ambitious, but with an unfortunate weakness for drink. Nevertheless, I had hopes that he would rise to be an asset to our firm once he had outgrown the follies of his youth.

It is not entirely clear what went on that night, but later witnesses said that Raven also joined the game at some point during the evening. Around midnight, a dispute broke out, with Kopek accusing Raven of cheating to win a hand. In the ensuing brawl, Kopek received a bloodied nose and left, threatening revenge. Some hours later, Raven was sleeping off the night's excesses at his lodgings in rooms opposite our warehouse when a mysterious fire broke out. Raven was burned alive in his bed and the following day Kopek was arrested on charges of arson and murder. He hanged himself rather than face a lifetime in prison. And that, under any normal circumstances, would have been that: a terrible tale of two wasted lives. But I now realise this was just the beginning.

It was the night-watchman at our new warehouse who first noticed something amiss. A dead rat outside the office door, sucked clean of blood and guts as if someone had inhaled the insides: a most unnatural sight. The next night he found a stray dog similarly emptied of life. At first, we dismissed these things as the work of a practical joker, but then the noises began. Strange knockings in the dead of night; footsteps clicking over empty cobbles and soon afterwards more tangible incidents: boxes and cases toppling over in the warehouse with no apparent cause. But whenever my watchman arrived with his lamp, there was no one there.

He was an honest fellow, and not one given to wild imaginings, but after a week the poor fellow's nerves were in such a state that he pleaded with me to let him go. His replacement lasted just three days, such was his agitation at the nightly events.

By now gossip was getting around of something dreadfully wrong at the warehouse: that the place where Kopek had worked had been somehow cursed by Jack Raven as he died. I did my best to dampen down the more fantastic talk, but already I was finding it difficult to persuade people to work there. One night I lost some valuable stock when thieves, chancing their luck, took advantage of a time when the building was unguarded.

I was determined to get to the bottom of the matter and so, armed with lantern and pistol, I took over the night watch myself. On the first evening, nothing happened. It was the same the following night. I began to feel extremely foolish. Perhaps the whole thing was nothing more than fanciful imaginations stirring up ghostly tales in the wake of a gruesome death? It was a little after midnight on the third evening when I realised that this was not the case at all. From the heart of the empty building, I heard the sound of footsteps. When I looked closer, moving out of the shadows towards me, I saw the figure of Jack Raven. The sea captain was as large as he was in life, but his face and body were bloodied and raw, his skin burned from his bones. I stared at the figure, unable to move, petrified by the sight of this horrific apparition. Then it tilted back its great head and let out the most appalling howl.

That noise will live with me until my dying day. Even as I write these words, I can feel the hairs on my neck rising at the memory of it. It was a scream of rage, anger and loss that froze me like a statue. Then, as I watched, the figure began to hurl great packing cases to the floor, smashing them open and scattering our valuable stock across the stones. This terrible rage continued for a full minute and then all was still. The figure had simply vanished, leaving behind utter destruction. I am a god-fearing man, Mr Ellison, and that night I believe I saw the devil himself.

What more to add to this terrible tale?

Nothing other than it has no conclusion. And so I write to beg for your help, Mr Ellison. There is no one else in Europe to whom I can turn. Jack Raven continues to haunt my warehouse. I cannot employ men to guard my stock, and

rumour and gossip are driving me to the edge of bankruptcy.
I have heard that the Cloven Pine has some special skill in
matters of this sort and I beg for your help now.

I have also heard something of your methods from my
associate in England, so I enclose with this letter some objects
that may be of use in your work. They were recovered from
the charred remains of Raven's room: a brass button from his
sea-coat; a medallion given to him by his dead mother on his
first sea voyage; some coins and a signet ring. I do not know if
any of these objects will be useful to you, but I sincerely hope
that you will look kindly on my situation. I am truly at my
wits' end and I hope to hear from you before the month is out.

I am, sir, your obedient servant,

Frans de Groot

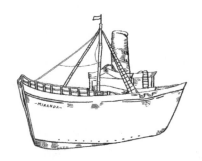

CHAPTER TWENTY-TWO

Ariel set down the letter on her lap and looked at her companions.

'That trunk is full of strange tales,' Dr Ellison said, tapping it with his foot, 'but we should be much encouraged. There is a great deal in that letter to help us. We know the name of our adversary, something which my great-grandfather always believed gave him power in any struggle. And I fancy we know far more about the motivations of this malevolent spirit than before.'

'The word "medallion" is underlined three times on the page,' said Ariel, looking at the letter again.

'Tobias had a habit of making notes in the margins, with thoughts and jottings about how he might proceed in a particular case. Charlie, you said you found some trinket inside the box of souls? A plain thing, nothing remarkable about it?'

'I added it to Bobby's jacket.'

Dr Ellison looked puzzled and Charlie explained how he had tied the medallion to the horse's winter coat back at Darkwater House.

'Then we must get it back quickly,' Dr Ellison said gravely. 'I suspect it may not be the sort of gift a horse or anyone else might want.'

'What do you mean?'

'The Cloven Pine often used objects as bait; objects that had a special significance to the spirit they were trying to capture. As metal conducts electricity, so they believed some things were capable of linking our world to theirs and Tobias became highly skilled at making the connections. I suspect he used that medallion to lure the spirit of Jack Raven into the box of souls, trapping him inside for all eternity. That is, until you two let him out.'

'And now his spirit has been gathering strength again,' Charlie said. 'But why is he looking for the medallion?'

Dr Ellison shifted in his chair. 'The letter suggests it was important to him in life: a link to the mother he had lost. Grief is a powerful thing. And so is rage at all those years of imprisonment. But at least we now know who he is and what he wants. It falls to us to seal Raven back inside that prison house: he cannot be allowed to rampage around this town any longer.'

'How do we do it?' asked Ariel.

'We must use the methods of Tobias and his society. He wrote about meeting your enemy on neutral ground if possible.'

'Where would that be?' Charlie asked.

Dr Ellison rose stiffly from his chair and moved once more to the window. Night had long since fallen and the children could see his stern expression reflected in the pane.

'This must end where it began. The sea, the headland and the lighthouse have all been entwined in this business from the start. The lighthouse tower is well away from the town and its people, whom we must not mix up in this affair any longer. We must face this spirit out there and end this tonight.'

He turned from the window and looked at them both intently.

'My great-grandfather writes time and time again in his journals about the need for curiosity and an open mind, and the great reserves of courage required to succeed in this line of work. You two have those qualities in abundance: you even possess that rarest of abilities to tune in and hear voices from the past. And I am too old and slow to do this on my own. The danger we face when we confront the spirit will be very real. Will you help me?'

Charlie exchanged a glance with Ariel. He could see a tiny spark flickering in her eyes and realised they had been through too much together, seen too much, felt too much, to step away now. He began to smile, and Ariel grinned back at him.

'Shall I take that as a yes?' the doctor asked.

'Yes!'

'Then I declare the Cloven Pine back in business,' Dr Ellison said. 'I confess I can feel a stirring in my old bones at the prospect of an adventure such as this. Come then. We have much to prepare.'

CHAPTER TWENTY-THREE

The clock struck ten as they stepped out into the snow. A full moon hung in the sky, circled by a bright ring of frost, and a bitter wind blew in fitfully from the sea.

Dr Ellison, dressed in a thick overcoat and boots, led the way, torch in one hand and his stick in the other. The cousins carried rucksacks on their backs. They had packed these with care, under the doctor's supervision: seven candles wrapped in a piece of embroidered cloth that he had taken from Tobias's trunk; a box of matches; a thermos of tea and, nestling in the bottom of Charlie's bag, a new box of souls.

He could feel the weight of the box pulling down on his shoulders as they walked, and at times it seemed as if it were ringing, as if this ancient object were somehow signalling its presence on a strange frequency that intermittently crossed the range of his own ear. He felt uneasy at the thought of it humming away on his back, a beacon for whatever else might be out there, tuning into its siren song.

They passed a cluster of cottages, scattered along the edge of the field like dice thrown by a giant hand. Christmas lights glowed in the windows and every now and then Charlie was able to look between the curtains at the lives inside: a man dozing in a chair bathed in the electric light of a television screen; a lady stirring cocoa in a striped blue mug; a child in pyjamas, yawning on its mother's lap. When he saw them, Charlie wished he could swap places with them all, but he forced himself to focus on the task ahead. Beside him, Ariel wore an expression of silent determination; he knew her well enough now to know that she was revelling in the night's adventure. This was life as she needed it to be: vivid, intense and beyond the ordinary. He drew courage from her example and pressed on with renewed concentration. Very soon, every detail of the brickwork of the passing cottages, every frosted garden, each crunching footstep made the world seem sharper to Charlie than at any other moment he could recall.

The distant lights of Dunstrand shimmered in the

darkness at the far end of the beach as Dr Ellison led them towards a crumbling barn, set a little back from the path.

'Ariel, open up, please.'

He tossed over a set of keys and gestured at the padlock. Ariel bent over the lock for a moment then dragged open the heavy door. Dr Ellison stepped into the darkness and flicked on a light switch. In front of them was an enormous red pick-up truck with huge wheels and a row of spotlights fixed above the driver's cab. The chrome bumpers gleamed as brightly as the yellow and orange flames which had been stencilled along the edges of the bonnet and doors. The children looked at him, astonished.

He was unapologetic. 'How else did you think I used to tow my boat? Come on. Climb in.'

Dr Ellison hauled himself up into the driving seat using the footplate and waved to the children to follow. He turned the key with a gleam in his eye.

'Hold on tight!'

The engine roared into life and the doctor eased the truck out of the barn onto the rough track towards the headland and the lighthouse. They bounced along, but after a few minutes their driver stopped at a fork in the road.

'We must not get too close to Darkwater,' said Dr Ellison, peering into the night, his hands steady on the wheel. 'We should not bring the box of souls and the medallion too close together until we are ready.'

'Why?' asked Charlie.

'The boxes amplify the effect of the bait. If we bring the two together before we are properly prepared, we risk alerting our adversary before our trap is set. We must separate here momentarily. I shall take the box up to the lighthouse to prepare things there. You two must go back to Darkwater to get the medallion. Leave your rucksacks with me.'

'Are you sure you'll be OK?' asked Charlie.

Dr Ellison's eyes were kind. 'Surely I should be asking that of you.'

'We'll be as quick as we can,' said Ariel. 'Good luck!'

'And you too. Be brave. We will end this business tonight.'

They watched the truck sway down the snowy track towards the headland and the lighthouse, red brake lights receding into the night. They stood for a moment under the stars, then switched on their torches and tramped in the opposite direction towards Darkwater House.

There were no lights on as they turned into the drive and hurried through the silent garden, buried in deep snow. A deer had left fresh tracks on the lawn and Charlie felt the black windows of the house watching them as they made their way round to the outbuildings. Never had the place felt so silent and lifeless, and he was grateful for Ariel's presence close by, leading the way with her torch and moving with purpose and calm. All his senses still felt heightened, as if his entire body had been plugged into the mains, crackling with an energy that was thrilling and terrifying all at the same time. They made their way round to the stable box. The door was open and there was no sign of the horse.

'Hey Bobby,' Ariel called softly. 'Where are you boy?'

'Shouldn't he be in here?' Charlie asked.

Ariel shrugged. 'The Coopers are pretty relaxed about him wandering up between our paddock and their fields. He knows his way around. But he normally comes in to one place or the other if it gets too cold or wet.'

They stood listening for a moment and then Ariel called out again into the night. The silence lay heavily around them. Charlie bit his lip and twisted the heel of his boot into the snow. Ariel picked up the feed bucket from beside the wall and shook it loudly. 'Hey Bobby. Want to get something to eat? Where are you, boy? Come here.'

He could see the concern in her eyes. 'Do you think something might have happened to him?' he said, beginning to voice what they were both starting to dread. 'Could the poltergeist have got to him? Surely he's too big to...'

'Bobby's probably up at the farm,' Ariel interrupted quickly. 'Maybe when David saw the weather forecast, he decided to keep him in up there. But Bobby's been spending so much time down in the paddock here lately that I—'

From out in the darkness there came the faint whinny of a horse. Charlie felt a wave of relief surge through his body.

'Hello, boy!'

Bobby trotted towards them and they both fell upon him, patting his nose and stroking his flanks, glad of his warm presence on this coldest of nights.

'You do like to wander off, don't you boy? You had me worried for a minute.'

'I think it may have been very good that Bobby's been on the move,' said Charlie. 'He has made it much more difficult for anyone to find him. Or anything.'

Ariel nodded. She led the horse towards the stable and switched on the light so that they could inspect his winter jacket. There, nestled among the trinkets and embroidered decorations, was the thin metal medallion that Charlie had tied to it a few nights before. He hesitated, suddenly fearful to touch it. When he did so, his cold fingers fumbled unsuccessfully with the knot. Ariel helped him and when he finally stuffed it into his pocket, he felt a sudden anxiety sweep over him.

'No going back now,' he whispered.

Bobby began to stamp his hooves and shake his mane back and forth in agitation.

'What's the matter with him?' said Charlie.

Ariel patted the horse's flank soothingly. 'I don't know,' she said. 'He's usually very calm. They sense stuff, horses. Something's disturbed him.'

'Perhaps he's not used to being ridden in the middle of the night?'

Ariel frowned and threw a riding helmet over to Charlie. 'Perhaps. Come on. Buckle up. You ready to ride?'

He nodded.

'You've come a long way, city boy.'

She swung herself into the saddle and helped
Charlie up behind her. It looked a big drop to
the ground.

'Did you tell me you'd never been on a
horse before?'

He nodded again. 'Never. I was supposed to once
on a school trip, but I pretended to be sick so I could
get out of it. I didn't use to like animals much.'

'And now?'

'Just show me what to do.'

'It's easy. Hold on tight and close your eyes.'

Ariel kicked her heels and they trotted out into
the yard and down the track behind the house.
Charlie gripped his cousin's waist and clenched his
teeth. After a few minutes he could see the fringe
of the dunes, dusted white with snow. Bobby picked
his footing carefully as the path dropped down to
the sand. There they paused, taking in the vista
before them.

The tide was going out and the beach was empty.
The full moon cut a path through the dark sea and
bathed the rock pools in silver light. Here and there
along the dunes, patches of snow glistened where
they had escaped the surging salt water and in the
distance the waves churned and hissed.

The horse tensed like a sprinter on the blocks, assessing the task ahead. Charlie squeezed his cousin's waist tightly to let her know he was ready. Then, with a wild shriek, Ariel kicked the horse into a gallop and they were racing away into the night.

It seemed to Charlie that they were flying, the icy air making his eyes water and blurring the boundary between land and sky. Seawater splashed up from the horse's hooves and trickled down his face as they raced over the sand, hurtling along under the bright moon. Charlie felt he had never travelled so fast. Ariel's body was set forward, at one with the horse, perfectly balanced, guiding Bobby with skill and determination towards the lighthouse. The hooves thudded into the damp sand and the horse was blowing hard now as the tower grew closer. Then they slowed, gradually at first, now more abruptly as Ariel leaned back towards Charlie and the horse gave a snort of pleasure and relief. Charlie unclenched his grip and gratefully patted the animal's steaming flank.

'There's Dr Ellison's truck,' Ariel pointed to the back of the beach and the headland.

The vehicle was parked about a hundred metres away on a scrubby patch of open ground. The snow was thinner there and they made good progress along the path before dismounting and hitching the horse to the gatepost.

'We'll be back soon, I promise,' Ariel told him. 'Good boy.'

The final walk on foot to the lighthouse seemed to take an age and at every step Charlie felt more vulnerable as they crossed the open ground.

'The entrance is round the far side,' said Ariel. 'I hope Dr Ellison has had enough time to get everything set up.'

The old stones of the lighthouse gleamed white under the moon. As they rounded its base, the crash of the waves grew louder.

'That's weird,' said Charlie. 'I thought he would have been out here to meet us.'

'Maybe he's inside.'

'Maybe.'

Charlie shone his torch around them, but there was no sign of the doctor. With a rising sense of alarm, he edged around the curve of the lighthouse wall. The torn sleeve of his coat scratched against the stone and his light picked out his own hesitant feet as he came closer to the doorway, growing ever more fearful of what he might discover around the other side. Then his beam picked out the entrance and illuminated something on the ground beside the threshold. Charlie's hand trembled as he tried to focus the light, sending a jerky shadow dancing over the doorway. He took in a swift, sharp breath. Something bulky was stretched out by the steps.

Dr Ellison's body lay face down, a trickle of blood running from his forehead and into the snow.

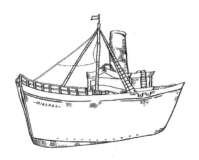

CHAPTER TWENTY-FOUR

They ran to the body.

'Dr Ellison – it's me, Charlie. Can you hear me?' He shook the old man's shoulders gently. 'He's moving.'

The doctor's face and eyelids twitched. Carefully, they helped him to a sitting position and he leaned against the lighthouse wall, his right hand pawing at his chest. Ariel wiped at the blood with her glove. A vivid red streak marked his hair and beard.

'He wants something from his pocket,' she said.

Charlie fumbled with the buttons on the old man's coat and pulled out a small flask.

Ariel sniffed it. 'It's whisky,' she said it. 'Give him some.'

She tilted back Dr Ellison's head and Charlie tipped a little into his mouth. The doctor coughed, then took another sip, swallowing with difficulty and slowly moving his neck from side to side. His eyes began to clear, but his voice was weak.

'Children, forgive me. I have underestimated the strength of our adversary. I fear I have led us all into great danger tonight.'

'What happened?'

Dr Ellison closed his eyes. 'After I left you, I transferred everything into my own bag, including the box of souls. I saw and heard nothing untoward. Then, as I set foot inside the lighthouse, there was a sudden rush of air around me and I was struck a tremendous blow on the side of my head. The next thing I knew I was lying in the snow with you two kneeling over me. I am too old to be of use tonight – and too foolish.'

Charlie shone his torch into the night around them. 'Where do you think it is now?'

'Close by, regathering its strength. Watching us.' Dr Ellison struggled to raise himself. 'This must end now. Run away, both of you. You must not stay here. Our enemy is too powerful and I am too weak to undertake the same feats as my great-grandfather. I have deluded myself, reading those old tales all these years. Flee while you can! Leave me and get far away from here.'

The effort of speaking seemed to exhaust him and

he fell back, his head lolling to one side, his breath coming shallow and fast.

'No way, Dr Ellison,' Charlie said firmly. There could be no running away, not now. Not after everything that had already happened.

'What do we have to do, Dr Ellison?' Ariel whispered. 'Tell us what we have to do and we'll finish this.'

'It's too dangerous,' the old man mumbled. 'I won't have it.'

'Dr Ellison, your great-grandfather drowned out there to keep this town safe. You owe it to him – we all owe it to him – to finish his work. Please. Tell us what we need to do.'

He closed his eyes for a moment. Below them, the sea ground against the rocks of the headland.

'All right,' he said slowly. 'All right.'

The children leaned close to hear his faltering voice.

'Take yourselves up to the lamp room at the top of the tower. You will find a stone pedestal in the centre where the oil lamp once stood. As Tobias would have done, lay down the cloth which we brought with us from the trunk. Place the box of souls on that, then set the seven candles in a ring around it and light them, just as he describes doing in his journals. Only then can you bait the trap.'

'With the medallion? OK. What do we do with it?'

A rueful smile curled at the edges of Dr Ellison's lips. 'Every situation is different and my great-grandfather's papers are sometimes a little vague on precise details. I expect you will know what to do with it when the time comes. You have the courage and curiosity. That's a good start.'

Charlie raised his eyebrows.

'What about you?' said Ariel.

'Leave me. Time is short and you have much to do. Do not worry on my account. Our enemy will soon return and be ready to strike. Make haste!'

Charlie got to his feet and grabbed the rucksack from the snow while Ariel stayed crouching beside Dr Ellison for a moment longer, looking into his eyes with concern.

'Go!' the old man whispered fiercely.

She squeezed his hand and joined Charlie at the lighthouse door. The doctor, still slumped against the wall, raised an arm in a weak salute. They began to climb the stairs, Ariel leading the way.

Inside, their footsteps echoed round the lighthouse tower, their torches illuminating each smooth step. Charlie thought of all the boots that had worn away the stone beneath his feet down the years, and of the furious storms and beating sun which had weathered the rocks outside. It was a way to help control the fear that was rising rapidly inside him and threatened to overwhelm him at any moment. His fingers closed nervously around the medallion in his pocket. It felt curiously warm, but he dared not stop to examine it. At a slit window halfway up the tower, the stars gleamed. The wind was blowing in fits and starts, each gust sending a strange moaning sound curling round the staircase and down into the dark.

'Will it come after us do you think?' Charlie said suddenly, startled by the sound of his own voice. Ariel reached back to brush his hand but said nothing. A moment later they were at the top.

Hurriedly, Charlie pointed his torch around the walls and floor. The room was empty apart from some startled rodent which scurried away into the gloom. As their eyes grew accustomed to their new surroundings, they could see the stones around them were streaked with dirt. In the centre, like an altar in a church, stood the wide stone platform that Dr Ellison had described. Beyond it was a gaping hole of a window, covered with a rusting wire mesh, which looked down onto the Serpent's Tongue rocks and the foaming sea. An ancient black bell hung on the wall beside them.

'Let's get this over with,' said Ariel briskly. She tugged at the straps of the bag while Charlie held the torch beam steady. She took out the candles, matches and cloth and began to arrange them as Dr Ellison had instructed. Charlie helped lay out the cloth, smoothing down the symbol of the Cloven Pine which was embroidered on it. Next, they set the candles in a ring upon the cloth and lit them. When that was done, Charlie removed the box of souls from the bag. Ariel placed it in the centre of the candles with its lid wide open. Perhaps it was a trick of the shadows, but to Charlie it seemed as if the inside of the box glowed with a faint blue luminescence, pulsing gently like a heartbeat.

'What do we do now?' he asked.

'Bait the trap, I guess. Have you got it?'

Charlie rummaged inside his coat pocket and pulled out the medallion. A gentle heat radiated from it, as if someone had recently been wearing it around their neck, and it swung slowly on its chain.

'Go on.'

Hesitantly, he took a step forward and lowered the little disc into the box of souls. It touched the bottom with a click and the chain coiled down on top. Charlie stepped back, half expecting something dreadful to happen, but other than a faint murmur of the wind, all was silent. They stood for a moment, still as the stone around them.

'Well what do we do if—'

'Shh!' Ariel held up her hand. 'Listen!'

Somewhere in the darkness a voice was whispering.

'*Call his name… Call his name…*'

'Can you hear that? Who is it?'

'I don't know. I don't recognise the voice at all.'

'Give me the light,' she said, taking the torch and sweeping it round the empty room. The instruction came again, faint and far away.

'*Call his name… Call his name…*'

'Someone is trying to help us,' said Charlie quietly. 'It's like hearing the ghost children, but it's not them this time. It's someone else…'

'*Call his name… Call his name…*'

Suddenly Charlie understood. At the top of his voice, he shouted: 'Jack Raven! We know who you are! We know what you want! We have it here! Come and take it! Show yourself to us if you dare!'

His words reverberated around the tower. For a

moment it seemed that the sound was echoing not just here and now, but back through all the years the lighthouse tower had stood guarding this ancient coast, back to the days when the oil lamp burned and the steamships braved the treacherous waters.

Ariel's face was alert, her senses straining.

'It's getting colder,' said Charlie. He moved towards his cousin and held her arm.

The candles around the box of souls guttered. One went out. Everything was silent for a moment and then there came the unmistakable sound of a footstep on the stairs. Then another. And another.

'He's coming.' Charlie squeezed Ariel's arm tightly. 'Jack Raven is coming.' With two hands to steady the beam, Ariel kept her torch light focused firmly on the top of the stairs. The footsteps were steady and unhurried, each one louder than the last. Instinctively the cousins edged back until Charlie could feel the mesh at the window press against his neck.

The old bell on the wall rang a single chime. They both jumped in alarm and the footsteps grew louder, much closer to the top of the stairs now. Then, abruptly, they stopped.

The children gripped one another tighter.

'What's happening?' Charlie whispered.

'I don't know.'

Another of the candles spluttered and went out.

Their breath steamed now, as if they had stepped into a freezer. Ariel shivered but held the torch steady.

Something was in the doorway.

Coming into focus at the head of the staircase, like a photograph developing in a darkroom, was the figure of a man. A pair of dead, empty eye-sockets stared out at them from a scorched and bloodied face.

Charlie's throat tightened; Ariel gasped and dropped the torch. The beam danced crazily on the ceiling as the torch rolled away noisily over the flagstones.

The figure stood silent, watching them.

It was Charlie who found his voice first.

'We know who you are, Jack Raven. We know what you did and what happened to you. We also know what you have been searching for. The medallion your mother gave you is right there.' His finger shook as he pointed at the box on the platform.

The figure did not move.

Charlie took half a step forward.

'It's yours, if you want it. Go on. Take it.'

The figure took a pace forward, the dead eye-sockets boring into Charlie's brain. Then Charlie felt a strange, churning sensation sweeping through him, a violent shock as if he had been pushed underwater by an enormous wave. He called out, but no sound came. As he looked at the burnt flesh and black eyes, he felt himself enveloped by the tide of anger and fury emanating from the apparition before him. He could feel Jack Raven's rage coursing through his own body and then, for a fleeting moment, he caught a sense of something else: a deep sadness, misery and wretchedness. Then as quickly as it had come, that sensation was gone and the all-consuming hatred burned around him again.

Through the confusion he heard a voice, the same faraway whisper as before: *'Talk to it, Ariel… Connect with it… You alone can understand its pain…'*

But before his cousin could respond, Charlie's feet lifted from the floor. He felt himself whirled around as if he were in a hurricane, and the walls and ceiling seemed to bend and sway around him. Then he fell, plummeting to the hard flagstones below. Peering up from the ground, he saw the figure of Jack Raven striding towards him, eyes blank, face twisted, fist raised ready to crack Charlie's skull like an egg.

———◇———

'Stop! Jack Raven, I command you to stop!'

The voice comes like a thunderclap, booming out around the lamp room. The figure freezes. Charlie blinks and although his vision is blurred he can see Jack Raven turn towards the centre of the room and the source of the voice. Charlie looks too, and his mouth hangs open in terror.

Ariel is standing on the stone platform, her arms stretched out like the wings of some great pre-historic bird, and a halo of white light shimmers around her. She looks older and taller. The box of souls blazes at her feet. The flames from the candles leap high at her sides, licking at her legs, but they do not hurt her. Her eyes shine with a fierce intensity.

Then the voice comes again, whispering advice once more.

'*Talk to it Ariel... connect with it...you alone can understand its pain...*'

Now her voice fills the room.

'Jack Raven! I know your name and who you are. You are a man of sin and a man out of your time and place. You must return to your prison house. You do not belong here.'

The figure raises its great fists and Ariel shakes her head.

'The time for your anger is over. You chose your own path in life and the consequences of those choices are yours alone. I know why you desire this.'

She holds the medallion out towards him.

'This was a token of your mother's love, given to you long before you embarked on your damned path, your violent life. But a mother's love endures. I, of all people, know that to be true.'

Her face softens.

'It is time to let go. It is time to leave this place. Come! Take what you desire and go. Be at peace, spirit. Be at peace.'

Slowly, the figure begins to sink to its haunches and for a moment Charlie thinks it is about to curl up on the floor. But then, as it crouches, he realises that it is gathering itself, fists clenched, ready to spring. He is too late to warn Ariel as, with a great roar, the figure leaps across the room towards the platform. Charlie screws up his eyes in anticipation of the sickening blow that he knows must come, and another wave of fury and rage sweeps over him with a sensation as tangible as if he were standing on a mountainside in a howling gale.

But the blow does not come.

Instead, when he opens his eyes, the figure is

paralysed, suspended in mid-leap as if captured in an oil painting. And Ariel, the box of souls burning at her feet, stands with her right hand outstretched, staring straight into the blank eyes and twisted face.

From the floor, Charlie is transfixed. He feels the rage and anger in the air around him subside and, in its place, that sensation again: a strange melancholy and sadness that makes the breath catch in his throat.

'Ah yes, Jack Raven!' Ariel's voice is calm now. 'I feel it too. I also know what it is to have a love ripped away. It is a fracture in the soul, but the time to rage against it is past. Be at peace.'

The figure, still frozen in front of her, looks back with those blank eyes.

'Take your medallion,' Ariel commands, 'and leave this time and this place forever.'

The grizzled head stares at Ariel. Then the figure clasps its hands over its face and lets out a howl of anguish and pain.

As the scream dies away, the figure regains the power of movement and steps forward to take the medallion from Ariel's hand. Its fingers close around the chain and it takes another step, this time into the strange fire burning around the box of souls. The flames rear up and for a moment the figure is entirely engulfed in their light. Then they fall back and the form of Jack Raven shimmers and shrinks, as if the very atoms of his existence are being compressed down into the box. Ariel kneels slowly and slams the lid shut. In that instant there is a blinding flash like lightning and a tremendous roar echoes round the room. Charlie buries his face in the floor.

———◇———

He did not know how long he had lain there, but when he looked up, the room was pitch black and silent. With an effort, he crawled across the stones, feeling for Ariel's torch. He found it after a few moments and switched it on. It flickered feebly into life and he swung the beam towards the platform.

'Ariel!'

His cousin was lying flat on her back, like a figure carved on a tomb. Clasped to her chest was the box of souls. Of Jack Raven, there was no sign at all.

'Ariel! Can you hear me?'

She was cold to his touch. With shaking fingers, he felt for a pulse at her neck. 'Come on, Ariel, please, please...' he mumbled to himself over and over.

Suddenly there was a footstep behind him.

Charlie whirled round.

Dr Ellison, pale and out of breath, was leaning against the doorway. 'Leave this to me,' he said.

'She's not breathing. I don't know what happened,' Charlie stammered.

Dr Ellison ran his hands down to Ariel's wrists to feel for a pulse, but they were wrapped too tightly around the box. With effort, he wrenched it from her and thrust it at Charlie.

'Run to the sea! Drown it deep.'

'But I want to help Ariel.'

'I am a doctor. This is my task. You are young and quick. The box is yours. Now go!'

On shaking legs, Charlie stumbled down the spiral staircase and clattered out into the cold night air. The snow lay all around, covering the headland. Ahead of him, the moon illuminated a path on the sea. He ran as he had never run before, legs numb with cold and fatigue, lungs burning. His mind was a jumble of visions and fragments from all he had witnessed. Then, amid all the confusion, he had a sudden second of clarity and could see himself from high above, a tiny black dot crossing a blank landscape, hurrying towards the water. He gripped the box of souls as tight as he could, fearful that it would fall from his hands and slither away into the night.

And then he was there, at the edge of the sea.

Charlie stopped, bending forward and fighting to regain his breath. His throat was raw and his eyes streamed from the cold. After a moment he straightened slowly and peered into the blackness.

Below him, the waves hissed over the fork of the Serpent's Tongue rocks. The white foam glimmered in the light of the moon, rising and falling with the flow of the tide. The smell of seaweed blew in on the wind. He took a couple of paces back from the edge and looked down at the box of souls.

He thought of the moment, less than a week ago, when he had discovered the first box. Now he barely recognised the lonely, homesick boy who had pulled it from the sand. So much had happened, so many incredible things.

For a second he hesitated. The box of souls was a thing of beauty, with its intricate design and strange history. It would be a shame for it never to see the light of day again. And then there was the extraordinary secret it contained. As if reading his thoughts, the box twitched in his hands. He shook himself, and with new determination, hurled it high into the air and out to sea.

The box flew in a graceful parabola over the water. For a split second it seemed to slow and catch the moonlight, spinning end over end, before tumbling down and hitting the water with a splash. Charlie saw the ripples spreading out in widening circles as the box bobbed for a moment and then sank from view. Exhausted, he fell to his knees and let out a long, slow breath, looking up at the stars. He knelt like that for several minutes until his limbs felt as if they would melt into the snow, and when he finally hauled himself to his feet, he was stiff and aching all over.

Then he remembered his cousin.

He ran, following his own tracks back to the lighthouse tower. He could barely lift his feet, but the thought of Ariel drove him on. He dragged himself up the stairs, gasping for breath and fearful of what he would find when he reached the top.

The candles were burning once more in the lamp room. The light was gentle and Dr Ellison stood beside the window. Propped up against the wall, his coat wrapped around her shoulders, was Ariel. She was drinking tea from the thermos flask. With the last of his strength, Charlie ran across the room and embraced her.

'Careful! You'll make me spill it.' Her voice was serene.

Dr Ellison beamed. 'She fainted, nothing more. But a nasty shock. For all of us.'

'I got rid of the box, like you said. It's at the bottom of the sea now.'

'Full fathom five,' murmured the doctor, 'where it should have stayed all along.'

Charlie took the flask and with unsteady hands, poured himself some tea. It was warm on his lips and he swallowed it gratefully.

'What happened to you, Ariel?' he said between gulps. 'It was...freaky.'

She shrugged. 'It's hard to explain. I remember we heard a voice telling us what to do and then after that...it was like I was watching myself in a dream.'

'You were different.'

Ariel frowned. 'I felt I was somewhere else entirely. And when the spirit attacked you, I suddenly knew it couldn't hurt me. I had what it wanted, I had the box of souls and I *understood* it. And in that moment, I knew I was more powerful than it could ever be.'

Dr Ellison put a hand on her shoulder. 'Tobias'

journals describe a sort of trance-like state that he could enter at times when the psychic energy was at its strongest. I never really understood what he meant, but I think I do now.'

'Empathy,' said Ariel. 'Tobias had the insight to try to understand these spirits, not fight them.'

'It was his voice we heard tonight,' Charlie said. 'I realised he was guiding us. Trying to help us.'

'You heard my great-grandfather?' Dr Ellison looked astonished. 'You two seem able to tune in to things the rest of us cannot. Extraordinary. How I wish I could have heard his voice as well.'

Ariel continued quietly: 'He understood Jack Raven was human once too. He knew he had lost his mother at a young age – that medallion was all he had to remember her by – and Tobias used that to capture his angry spirit all those years ago.'

Tears began to fill her eyes.

'What's the matter?' said Charlie.

'Just before I closed the box, I heard Tobias' voice again. He was very close to me and he was whispering just to me.'

'What did he say?'

'He told me to picture my mother, and suddenly I could see her as clearly as I see you both now. She was standing there beside me. And in the moment after the box was shut, she gave me the longest, tightest most amazing hug you could ever imagine. I know that she loves me and my dad and she always will. There is no anger in her. Only calm and forgiveness. She is at peace with the world and I must be too.'

The horizon was brightening by the time the three of them, leaning on one another for support, stepped out of the lighthouse and into the frozen air. As Dr Ellison climbed into the truck, Charlie and Ariel stood together for a moment in the snow, looking back at the lighthouse.

It was then that they saw him.

A little way off, standing beside the dunes with his face to the sea, was a tall man, dressed in a long black coat, his hair curling down to the collar. As they watched, he turned slowly and looked directly at them. Then he nodded gently and a tiny smile played at the corners of his lips. The voice that whispered over the snow was faint, but familiar.

'*Thank you. Thank you both...*'

They stood in amazement.

It was Charlie who first came to his senses. 'Dr Ellison!" he shouted. 'Come quickly! Come and see!'

They rushed back to the truck where the old man

was still settling himself into the driver's seat.

'What is it?'

'You have to come back. Now!'

Dr Ellison looked bewildered. 'Where?'

'Down on the beach. Come quick!'

The old man struggled out of the truck and, grumbling under his breath, slowly followed the children back towards the sea. But by the time he arrived at the spot where they had been standing, the dunes were empty, and the figure was nowhere to be seen.

CHAPTER TWENTY-FIVE

It was either the bang of the front door or the shout of greeting that woke Charlie; he wasn't sure which. He rolled over and blinked in the bright light that flooded into his attic room. He reached blearily for his phone, which told him it was already past midday. Yawning, he wandered downstairs to the kitchen, where Uncle Patrick was unpacking from his extended trip, piling cardboard boxes onto the table.

'Good afternoon, Charlie.' His uncle paused, looking him over suspiciously. 'Been at the Christmas sherry?'

'Not this morning.'

Patrick grinned and unzipped his overnight bag.

'Well, whatever you've been up to, I'm glad to see you've survived. It was all a bit Scott of the Antarctic out there yesterday, so I'm sorry I couldn't get home until now. The roads are better today, but when that blizzard first started... I've never seen anything like it. How have things been here? I couldn't help noticing that lots of the books in the study seem be on different shelves. And the cutlery. Most of it is in different drawers...

'We had a bit of a tidy-up,' said Charlie.

'Really?' His uncle looked doubtful.

But before he could press Charlie further, Ariel rushed into the room and embraced her father tightly. He hugged her back, faintly surprised.

'How was your trip?' she asked.

'A little longer than planned, but very successful, thank you. A white Christmas is good for business. What have you pair been up to? Boxing?' He peered at Ariel's cut lip and the bruise on Charlie's forehead, both legacies of the violent encounter in the alleyway the previous day. 'I'm well aware I'm supposed to be the responsible adult round here and that I may be failing in my duties. What on earth happened?'

Ariel unwound herself from her father's arms. 'Just a low branch,' she said quickly. 'Nothing for you to freak out about. We were out riding. I got caught too.'

Uncle Patrick narrowed his eyes. 'I thought Charlie didn't ride horses?'

'This is exactly why,' said Charlie brightly. 'Done it once now, but never again.'

Before Uncle Patrick could respond, they were distracted by the sound of a car pulling up outside.

'I think we have visitors,' he said. Charlie looked through the window and a smile spread over his face. Of course! With everything that had happened he had lost track of the days: it was Christmas Eve. Time to go home.

'Dad!' he shouted. 'And Mum's here too!'

He rushed outside as his mother stepped from the car. He clasped her long and tight, and for a second she looked puzzled at this unaccustomed display of affection.

'Let me look at you, Charlie,' she said, holding him at arm's length. 'There's plenty of colour in your cheeks. I told you the fresh air would do you good. But what have you done to your forehead?' She examined the bruise closely, as if her son were another of her A&E patients at the hospital. 'Just a bit of a bump by the look of it. I think you'll survive.'

'Believe it or not, Julia,' said Patrick, kissing his sister on each cheek, 'they tell me they did that when they were out horse riding.'

Charlie's mother's eyes widened. 'Charlie? He

normally runs a mile if animals are involved. You really must have had quite a week. Good for you.'

She hugged Ariel while Charlie's dad, his suntan incongruous against the winter trees, grabbed his son in a friendly headlock. 'I told you I'd come and pick you up! And your mum was desperate to come along too, when it came to it.' He lowered his voice to a whisper. 'Don't tell her I told you, but I think she missed you.' He looked up at the house, running an engineer's eye over its crooked walls. 'What a peculiar-looking place you've been hiding out in. Is the roof made of gingerbread?'

Charlie grinned. 'Nothing would surprise me round here.'

There were more hugs and handshakes and a confusion of kisses, coats and coffee mugs, and eventually they were all beside the Christmas tree with the children building a fire in the grate.

'You can't possibly head back tonight,' Patrick said, settling down beside his sister on the sofa. 'The roads are still bad.' Charlie's parents exchanged a glance.

'What do you think?' his mother asked her husband.

Charlie's father hesitated. 'We mustn't impose...'

'You wouldn't be imposing at all,' said Uncle

Patrick. 'And it's way too far to drive back with the weather like this. Stay tonight. Spend Christmas Day with us. It's no problem, honestly. We've got loads of room.'

Charlie caught sight of his father anxiously mouthing the word 'vegetarian' at his mum, and she laughed. 'Don't worry. I did take the precaution of bringing a few things along just in case the weather turned bad again – including the turkey. It's in the cool box. I've even got the mince pies and the stocking too. And a few presents.'

Charlie's dad looked relieved and spread his arms over the sides of his chair, as if physically embracing the new plans. 'Perfect! Just so long as you've got a decent pub round here, Patrick.'

They went to the supermarket in Dunstrand that afternoon to buy extra supplies for Christmas lunch. The narrow aisles were packed with last-minute shoppers. Ariel held her father's arm as they walked round and every now and then one of them would point at something on a shelf or at one of the harassed shoppers and they both would laugh. The hostility between father and daughter was melting away like snow in spring. Charlie watched them talking, his uncle's face a mixture of joy and grateful disbelief.

What would he say if he knew what had really happened? In Charlie's mind, the memories of the previous night were fading like a dream. He could still remember the cold and the fear, the gleam of the box and the strange transformation of his cousin as she stood amid the candle flames. Had she really seen her mother in that bizarre trance-like state? But he had witnessed so many extraordinary things over the past few days that he knew better than to dismiss even the most fantastic of notions, and the evidence of reconciliation between daughter and father was as real as the cobblestones over which they now walked on their way back to the car.

Charlie's mum stopped abruptly. 'We forgot the Christmas crackers!' She looked back at the supermarket with a shudder. 'I'm not going back in there. Can you two nip into that newsagent's for me, please? We'll put the shopping in the boot and come back and find you.'

Charlie and Ariel went into the shop and found what they needed. As they waited to pay, Ariel gave him a nudge and pointed to a copy of the *East Anglian Daily Times* in a rack by the counter. Charlie could make out the headline and the opening paragraph of the story beneath:

ANTIQUE DEALER TO MAKE 'FULL RECOVERY' AFTER MYSTERY BREAK-IN

Dunstrand antique dealer Arnold Cartwright, 62, is expected to make a full recovery from the head injuries he sustained during an attempted burglary at his shop, according to doctors. Mr Cartwright is conscious and has now been interviewed by police, who say he has no recollection of the attack. Police admit they have no leads in the case, but their enquiries are continuing. Cartwright's Antiques will re-open in the New Year with assistant manager Angela Timms expected to take over the running of the business for the foreseeable future...

———◇———

Charlie looked at his cousin and a little smile of a secret shared passed between them. Then, as they paid for the crackers, Ariel spotted something through the shop window. Grabbing his hand, she hurried him out into the street where Clara Cooper stood, deep in conversation with Miss Stanford. Pebble shifted in his harness at their approach and Clara turned her head in their direction. 'Ariel? Charlie?'

'Hello, Clara,' said Ariel, 'I've been meaning to ask you: how is Rose getting on?'

'Very much on the mend, thank you. The doctor says her arm will be out of the sling early in the new year. Children are very resilient at that age.'

'I still feel dreadful about the whole thing,' said Miss Stanford with a shudder. 'When I think what could have happened...'

Clara stroked her arm. 'It was an accident, my dear. Don't blame yourself. You have done more for the children of this town than anyone has done for many a long year. In fact, I hear some of the parents are already asking if we can have another concert at Easter. All this business will soon be forgotten.'

Miss Stanford looked hopeful. 'Do you think so?'

'I am certain of it.'

At that moment, Uncle Patrick and Charlie's parents reappeared across the square. Miss Stanford waved at Patrick and his face broke into a broad smile. He beckoned her over to join them for a drink in the Mariner's Arms and with a hurried goodbye, she crossed the street. The children held back from following them all, remaining with the old woman for a moment.

'You found Dr Ellison, I assume?' she said to

them quietly.

'Yes,' said Ariel, 'And we—'

Clara raised her hand. 'I don't need to know. In fact, I don't want to know. Just reassure me there's no need for any further concern.'

'None,' said Charlie firmly.

The old lady's face crinkled into a knowing smile. Gently, she touched each of their faces in turn. Pebble barked.

'You are courageous children,' she said. 'I wish you both a peaceful Christmas.'

From the other side of the square came the familiar beep of a horn and David, a sprig of holly tied to the headlamps of his tractor, gave them a thumbs-up from the cab.

'That must be my taxi,' she said. 'Give my love to everyone.'

Steadily and slowly, with Pebble at her side, the old lady made her way across the marketplace and disappeared among the Christmas Eve shoppers.

That night at Darkwater House, the family cooked and ate together, a fire blazing in the kitchen burner. And afterwards, by the light of the Christmas tree, they played cards until their eyes grew heavy. Charlie felt content, curled up on the sofa between his mother and father, the strange creaks of the house now sounding as soothing as the chatter of an elderly companion. The children hung their stockings beside the fireplace and went upstairs.

'How did you really get on up here this week?' Charlie's mum said, sitting at the end of his bed as he tucked down in the attic room. 'I'm not sure I would recommend you make a career as a jockey.' She leaned forward to rub the bruise on his forehead gently. His dad, watching from the doorway, yawned.

Charlie shrugged. 'It's been all right.'

'That's your verdict on everything,' said his mother, ruffling his hair. 'Can't you give me a little more to go on? I mean, Patrick tells me you two were stuck here on your own for a couple of nights in a blizzard. That must have been a bit alarming in a place like this.'

'Like what?'

'You know. Remote. Old. Weird.'

'Sounds just like your parents,' his dad said.

Charlie laughed. 'It was all...fine. Nothing much more to say, really.'

His mother kissed his cheek and his dad saluted from the doorway, his hand poised over the light switch.

'I'm very proud of you,' his mother said. 'I know it wasn't how you would usually choose to spend the start of your holidays. And I think it's been brilliant for Ariel to have you around.'

Charlie looked up at her smiling face. 'You know,' he said slowly, 'I think if I can get through the week I've had out here, then nothing's ever really going to bother me again.'

He thought for a second of Joe Dixon and his stupid gang of school bullies. Things would be different from now on. They suddenly seemed pathetic...inconsequential, even. And miles and miles away. 'Seriously, Mum, nothing at all.'

'I'm glad to hear it, Charlie. Sleep well.'

His dad turned out the light.

Charlie lay there for a while, listening to the wind curling round the sills and the hoot of a distant owl. He wriggled down deeper under the covers. But just as he was drifting off to sleep, there was a tiny knock at the door. It was Ariel, beckoning him silently to follow. With an effort, he hauled himself out of bed and followed her along the passageway.

They were outside the door of one of the empty bedrooms when Ariel gestured to stop. Charlie strained his ears in the silence and then, faintly,

Jim Cockin

he heard it: quiet at first, but growing louder, the unmistakable sound of two children laughing.

'They're back,' said Ariel. Her eyes gleamed.

'Back home where they belong,' said Charlie. 'Nothing prowling round the neighbourhood to frighten them away now. I wonder if my mum and dad will be able to hear them.'

Ariel shook her head. 'I don't think many of us can.'

'Tell me something,' said Charlie. 'Were you scared last night?'

'Terrified. But not at the end.'

'I thought you were very brave,' he said. 'What you did at the lighthouse was amazing.'

'I'm not really sure I did anything. It just sort of happened.'

'I wonder if it will happen again?'

Before his cousin could answer, the laughter behind the door rose to a new pitch and then faded away as if the owners were making their way to another place and another, more distant Christmastime. Charlie went back to his room and soon he was fast asleep.

———◇———

The morning dawned brighter and warmer than previous days, the snow dripping from the branches of the trees as the sun's rays touched them. After breakfast, the family gathered around the tree to open their presents. Charlie was excited to unwrap the football boots he had wanted all season; Ariel was delighted with her new riding jacket. Uncle Patrick then organised everyone into kitchen teams and set them to work around the stove peeling potatoes and carrots and preparing the sprouts and parsnips. The cousins quietly smuggled a few vegetables into their pockets and while lunch was cooking they slipped out to the stall in the courtyard behind the house to feed Bobby a Christmas Day treat. He crunched noisily on the carrots and shook his mane approvingly, none the worse for the previous night's adventure. Later, the family sat down to eat a long and happy lunch and afterwards they decided to take the slushy track down to the beach for a walk.

The tide was out when they got there and the sand was as wide and empty as it had been on the first day of Charlie's visit. The tide pools rippled in the breeze. The children walked a little way behind the adults, savouring the tranquillity of the day and the good lunch, each glad of one another's company and aware of the unspoken bond that had been forged between them by the strange events of their week together.

As they neared the headland, they saw a man leaning on the gatepost by the path. The adults passed him with no more than a nod as they climbed towards the lighthouse tower. But the children stopped. It was Dr Ellison.

'I'm so very sorry,' he said. 'So very, very sorry.'

'Why? Everything turned out all right in the end,' said Charlie.

'I should never have put you in such danger,' the old man replied.

'We should actually be thanking you,' said Ariel. 'If it wasn't for you, none of this would have been fixed.'

He looked at them sadly. 'This won't be the end of it. You know that, don't you? I don't mean Jack Raven. He won't trouble anyone again. But after one has shown a talent for dealing with this sort of trouble, it has a habit of seeking you out once more. Since our little adventure the other night, I have found myself wondering, why you two? And why now? I fear something very peculiar is happening and that the Cloven Pine may need to be more than just a footnote in history before all this is done.'

'Dr Ellison, if you don't mind me saying,' Charlie patted him on the arm, 'I think you're forgetting what a nasty shock you had the other night. It's bound to make you feel a bit odd. Try not to worry too much about it. It is Christmas Day after all.'

Dr Ellison smiled and stared at the lighthouse, the wind ruffling his hair. 'We live in an age of reason: the supremacy of science, the triumph of technology,' he said. 'We think we know and understand it all, but we don't. The same mysteries that have been at work in this world, haunting mankind since the beginning of time are still here with us – they are just harder to hear amid all the noise. But you two sense them. I can sense them – although not as strongly as you – and I foolishly tried to block them out over the years for fear of being labelled some sort of freak. But I am nearing the end now and when you reach my age there is no longer any point denying these things. The world is full of surprise and wonder: we forget that at our peril.'

The old man sighed and shook each of them by the hand.

'Forgive me. This day above all others is no time for morbid reflection. You are right. We all should be enjoying the moment we have before us now. A very Merry Christmas to you both.'

And with that, he set off back along the track in the direction of his cottage. Charlie and Ariel watched him go until he was nothing more than a dark dot under the vast sky.

'You know what?' said Charlie. 'I was thinking last night about how I found that box in the first place. It was over there when I was using that old metal detector. And then I realised something.'

'What?'

'I left it there. The metal detector is still behind those dunes over that ridge.'

They looked at one another with sly smiles.

'Didn't Dr Ellison say that his great-grandfather had a bag full of things he threw overboard when the ship sank?'

'Yes.'

'Which means there might have been more than one box that went into the water?'

'Possibly.'

Ariel glanced up at the lighthouse. The adults were almost at the tower, still deep in conversation. Then one of them must have realised the children were lagging behind, because they all turned and beckoned them to catch up.

'You know, I don't really think I can face going back inside that lighthouse again,' she said. 'I'm just going to pretend I can't hear them.'

'Me too.'

'Shall we see if we can find the metal detector instead?'

'Yes,' said Charlie. 'Maybe we could even have another go with it over the dunes.'

'That sounds an excellent idea. Where did you say you left it?'

Charlie pointed further down the beach.

'Come on.' Ariel smiled. 'I'll race you there.'

ACKNOWLEDGEMENTS

Much gratitude is owed to many people, without whom you would not be holding this book in your hands right now. Where to start?

Simon Trewin's enthusiasm for the first draft of *Ghost Tide* inspired me to continue working on the story and the shrewd suggestions of early readers Anne-Marie Conway, Janet Cockin, David Hall and Natalie Watts helped me to develop it further. Olivia Doughty and family provided constructive observations along the way.

Dan Hiscocks and the team at Lightning Books have been terrific partners from the moment they first took on the manuscript and I'm particularly grateful to editor Simon Edge for all his diligent and detailed work to improve the text, including introducing me to the extraordinary account of a real-life North Sea shipwreck in Sean Street's *The Wreck of the Deutschland*.

Richard Donoghue provided the design expertise to create the first map of Dunstrand which was then brilliantly brought to life by Martha Vine, who also provided the illustrations for the book, including the front cover. Thank you to Nell Wood for the cover design and layout of the text.

The magnificent public libraries in Hammersmith and Richmond played their part by providing quiet spaces to work (our libraries are places to cherish) and I'm also grateful to Magnus and Nadine Brooke and to Dom and Kirsty Shales who were all generous hosts in times of writing need. And, at the very last, Ashley and Sian Jouhar were there to put me in the picture. Special thanks also to my son Henry for his encouragement, inspiration and ever-patient tech tutorials.

But the biggest thanks must go to my wife Rebecca, who has been unfailing in her support for this book, and for me, from the very first word to the last. Without her expertise, knowledge, good humour and love, there really would be no book at all.